SCHWARZENEGGER
PREDATOR™

SOON THE HUNT WILL BEGIN...

TWENTIETH CENTURY FOX Presents

A GORDON · SILVER · DAVIS Production

ARNOLD SCHWARZENEGGER "PREDATOR" CARL WEATHERS

Music by ALAN SILVESTRI

Written by JAMES E. THOMAS & JOHN C. THOMAS

Produced by LAWRENCE GORDON, JOEL SILVER and JOHN DAVIS

Directed by JOHN McTIERNAN

DOLBY STEREO
IN SELECTED THEATRES
Color by DeLuxe

PREDATOR

A Novel by Paul Monette
Based on a Screenplay by James E. Thomas & John C. Thomas

A JOVE BOOK

PREDATOR

A Jove Book / published by arrangement with
Twentieth Century Fox

PRINTING HISTORY
Jove edition / June 1987

ISBN: 0-515-09002-6

Jove Books are published by The Berkley Publishing Group,
200 Madison Avenue, New York, New York 10016.
The words "A JOVE BOOK" and the "J" with sunburst
are trademarks belonging to Jove Publications, Inc.

PRINTED IN THE UNITED STATES OF AMERICA

To Roger Horwitz

Achilles was not such a warrior
nor so mourned by his comrade-in-arms

PROLOGUE

The predator woke slowly from the icy depths of his dream-state. As his consciousness returned in languid waves of recognition, the insular silence of his life-chamber softly echoed with the sigh of his breathing and the swift quadruple rolling of his heart, intense as a hummingbird.

A finger touched a smooth plate at the side of the console. Instantly the light in the cocoon chamber shifted from amber to blue as the stasis field—a modular pattern of strobing light-beams that hovered above his warrior's body, controlling his vital functions—dissolved, returning control of the ship once more to his command.

The light flow across the control panel fluttered, settling into familiar navigational patterns, analyzing and adjusting the craft's velocity to the constraints of the unexplored gravity field. Constantly decelerating, the ship began to ease into a steady, high-altitude orbit, where analysis of vital data on the watery planet far below would begin.

As the craft responded to the predator's adjustment of speed, altitude and parabola, his finger again touched the burnished plate on the console. A matrix of microscopic wire rose soundlessly, energized and began to glow, resolving into an electronic display screen. Information as to the planet's location in the solar system was entered. A high-speed display of data momentarily filled the screen, followed by a spectrum review of the planet's inhabitants, the predator's only guide to the alien species of the planet Earth.

Big cats, rhinos, bears, elephants—all passed in rapid review, accompanied by a biological analysis of each animal. Then primates appeared, and the images began to slow, holding on the image of a hairless, bipedal creature. The image expanded to full frame, becoming three-dimensional, as a more complex array of data flashed around the periphery of the screen.

A detailed, biomechanical analysis followed, indicating the range of the creature's varied and remarkable evolutionary adaptations to the planet. The predator touched the plate again, and the analysis shifted to an anatomical breakdown, peeling away, in layers, the muscular, organic, and skeletal composition. The brain followed, showing the left and right hemispheres and the quadrants relating to memory, speech, and motor activity.

A final touch to the plate and the encyclopedic screen filled with further configurations of the biped depicted in a variety of situations, then followed by an image totally unlike the others.

The predator leaned closer to the screen, studying the final image of this creature, dressed in camouflage and heavily armed with weapons strange in appearance but familiar in function and deadliness. Here was a creature modified and trained for a single function—to kill—exactly the creature the predator sought, the challenge worthy of his own vast skill, a kindred spirit at last, a reason to exist.

ONE

THE SHIVERING RED-ORANGE burn of the humid sun throbbed like a fever along the Pacific rim of the Conta Mana coast. The beach and shallow harbor at Balancan, deadly still in the late afternoon heat, nonetheless looked pristine as a travel poster with its limpid emerald water and white powder sand. The thatch huts of the fishing village were simple as an urbanite's dream of Eden, though inside every one was like an oven, stinking of rotten grass, the air thick with the whine of green-headed flies. You never lost the heat in Conta Mana in September, even at night, especially at night. It hadn't rained on the coast since June, and no one in Balancan was holding his breath. The heat was a given like being poor, or being shot by guerrillas.

Inland from the village, darkness was already thick in the trees, and the coastal jungle hissed and seethed like a pot of boiling water. A hungry cougar began to flex in his lair in anticipation of the chase, the rip of a boar's hide, the thick-clotted heart sweet as wild honey. Everything small and succulent—the mice, the ferrets, the blue-hair monkeys—plunged into their burrows and nests, giving over the night to a thousand snakes, a thousand kinds of venom. Nothing tender would still run free by morning.

Tangles of exotic flowers groped for the last of the light. Rotten orchids fell into jelly, trampled by sunflowers two feet across. Whatever bloomed exploded, aching with pollen. Jasmine ran riot like weeds, looped with snags of vines and reverberating with the screams of macaws and parrots, who flew in a green blaze of magic, erasing time. In every rush of their wings were conjured images of blood-soaked Mayan priests and nobles a thousand years gone, praying at their zigzag temples beyond Lake Panajachel.

And beyond the lake, at the humped spine of Conta Mana, the ominous black bulk of a dead volcano's peak pierced the last clouds of a thunderstorm riding east toward the highland jungles and out to the pale Caribbean.

Then suddenly, like a siren in a dream, the timeless balance of Balancan was invaded by the sputtering blades of a helicopter, a huge U.S. Army assault chopper slapping the heavy air as it approached the village. It hovered above the huts along the shore, rippling the matted roofs, seeming to watch like an alien ship, absurdly incongruous in the primitive setting, till just as abruptly a ring of landing lights flicked on in the close-cropped field beyond the huts. Three puffs of pale blue smoke rose from a tin chimney in the largest hut. The UH-1H chopper sank toward the field.

As it fanned the grass its whacking blade kicked up violent swirls of heavy dust, sending a pair of rutting monkeys scurrying and screeching into the brush. Yet no native children ran and hid behind the banana trees; no women looked up from their looms; no peasant farmer bent for a ladle of water from a clay jug.

But the helicopter's landing was watched most closely, by a uniformed man with a twitch in his jaws who stood silently behind a window of the main hut. General Homer Phillips was top man of the Balancan command, a place that had stopped being a fishing village ten years ago. At fifty-five, Phillips was a hardened, tough lifer, canny and methodical like the jungle hunters prowling in the wild coastal forest around him. His nameplate and insignia were routine Army, and the braid on his chest showed his steady rise from infantry corporal, cutting his teeth in the ditches of Da Nang. Only a thin pale silver bar in his collar identified his special unit: Code 4 BRAVO. They were the elite of the elite commandos—post-Vietnam, post-Beirut. Homer Phillips and his men fought the newest kind of war in the oldest kind of way.

Even before the chopper's skids touched ground, the sliding door of the aircraft was hurled open. The first man to appear was dressed in fatigues and armed with full combat gear, belt studded with ammunition, a sheathed machete swinging at his right side. As he leaped from the chopper he seemed as massive as a linebacker, yet as quick on his feet as a hurdler. His blond hair was clipped low, and his eyes were steel gray and level as a falcon's. His ruggedly handsome face was totally alert, totally ready. As he hit the ground running he barked an order over his shoulder, the words all swallowed by the roar of the engine.

The general lowered the bamboo shade on the window and turned back to the room. "He's here," he said curtly to a soldier who was working at a desk in the dim light a few feet away, as if the soldier hadn't heard the chopper land. Mostly the general sounded relieved.

Meanwhile, several men ran out from various huts in the camp even before the rotors on the UH-1H had stopped slicing the air. Heads were lowered, and hands covered mouths as protection from the choking dust still swirling in the air. There was apparently no time to waste. The detachment of Conta Mana regulars who were cooperating with the Americans quickly began to transfer equipment from the vibrating UH-1H, landing it onto a hoist and moving it across to a pair of smaller assault helicopters silently standing by at the clearing's edge.

The man in fatigues strode through this flurry of activity and urgency, heading for the main hut. He stopped on the porch, pulled a cigar from his shirt pocket, and struck a match on his thumbnail. Major Dutch Schaefer had been through every jungle outpost the Army could think up, and the wildness of the territory never seemed to ruffle his demeanor. He might look like a football hero from the Midwest, but he had a street kid's surly underlip, and something in him was wilder than any jungle. If he was weary from constant duty, he didn't show it. He seemed on guard like a watchdog waiting to spring into action, his instincts so highly tuned he could hear a leaf rustle ten meters away in his sleep. But he always had time to stop and light a cigar.

Schaefer turned to watch the men move the equipment, casting an appraising eye on the assault choppers. The hoist lurched past him, its engine growling and skipping at the insult of the crude petrol available in this backwater of the world. Night was now quickly overtaking the village, at a pace only possible in the tropics, where a curtain of darkness dropped as if every day was the end of a play. Then, as if a switch had been turned on, the cool night breeze blew in from the harbor and started to give some relief to the overheated village.

As Schaefer walked into the hut, Phillips stepped forward into the dim light cast by a lone naked bulb hanging over a desk littered with maps. As the two men exchanged the briefest smile, enormous moths attacked the bulb like miniature warplanes mimicking an air raid.

Then the major informally saluted the general, who was not only Schaefer's senior in rank, but two wars older.

"You're looking well, Dutch," Phillips said warmly as he returned the major's salute, then immediately reached forward and grasped his shoulder. It was a gesture of respect.

"I make sure they feed me good," Schaefer replied with a wry grin as the two men descended a flight of stairs into the basement command post. They walked quickly through a tunnel lined with radio equipment, then ascended again into the palapa, a large, two-room shed with a concrete floor and thatched walls and roof. Here was where the assault choppers had been stored. Behind a partially drawn curtain another bare bulb was strung from the rafters, illuminating a bank of compact field radio gear, maps, and stacks of infrared aerial photographs, all of it as incongruous in the primitive place as the chopper had seemed minutes before.

A sense of urgency was mutually understood from the start. It was time to get to work. Schaefer was as always energized by the thought of a raw challenge, taut as a whip and itching to be presented with an impossible assignment. He was a tough, effective combat man who preferred to lead the front lines, where he could test his physical and mental strength against the worst odds. He didn't yet know why he had been summoned here with such immediacy, but he knew already that if Phillips was involved, it must be the heavy guns.

"We've got ourselves one hell of a problem here," Phillips said, pointing at a topographical map that was edge to edge with deep jungle. "Somethin' right up your alley." He leaned close to the map where it trailed through the Guatemalan highlands near the mouth of the Usamacinta, circling a set of coordinates in the pale green along the Conta Mana border. It seemed like the middle of nowhere. No roads, no villages marked, nothing.

"Eighteen hours ago," Phillips began, "we got word that one of our choppers was down. It was transporting three cabinet members of this charming little country— don't ask me where, don't ask me why. All we know is it was shot down right here," he said, pointing to the tiny circled area on the map. "The pilot radioed from the ground that they were all alive. Their position was fixed by the transponder beacon onboard. Right here," he said again, tapping the location repeatedly, as if he could jog loose some feature of the place, something to make it make sense.

Schaefer studied the map carefully for a half a minute, then looked up at Phillips. "That's over the border, General," he said flatly.

Phillips furled his brow. "Probable," he said with a curl of distaste. "Very fucking probable. Apparently, they strayed off course. We're pretty certain they've been scooped up by the guerrillas."

Schaefer puffed on his cigar. "What have you got in mind, General?"

"We figure we got less than twenty-four hours to

catch up with them," he replied. "After that, not much hope. They'll realize they don't really need them alive. They'll be heroes if they kill three politicians. So we want a rescue operation mounted tonight. Which doesn't give you shit for time."

"What else is new," Schaefer commented dryly, inhaling on the cigar again. "Rescue three scumbag politicians, make the world safe for democracy. When do we leave?"

"You lift off in three hours," Phillips answered, looking at his watch. "Oh, there's one other thing."

"Oh, yeah? Gee, I can hardly wait." Schaefer chuckled. "One other thing is usually the pipe bomb in my sleeping bag."

"Someone else will be going with you," came the response.

Schaefer's body tensed imperceptibly, and his eyes narrowed slightly. He stubbed the cigar out in an ashtray. "You know we don't work with outsiders, General," he said tightly. "It's just me and my home team. Think of us like the Celtics."

As Schaefer spoke, another man entered the room in time to hear his reply. "Who said anything about outsiders, Dutch?"

Schaefer turned. It was Al Dillon, a career intelligence man with whom Schaefer had shared special services duty in Thailand years before. Now in his mid-thirties, Dillon had grown up in South Central L.A., the only kid of color who'd made it off his block for good. He knew the violent ways of the coke-war streets, where his combat training started as soon as he could walk.

Dillon was dressed in new jungle fatigues with the

creases still in them, and holding a sheaf of papers. Although as rugged and hardened-looking as the other soldiers, his bearing and grooming indicated he'd been away from the business of soldiering for a while. In a way he was the whitest man in the room. He had obviously traded in his last fatigues for a desk job, and that made Schaefer very, very wary. To Schaefer a bureaucrat was a lowlife, no matter how high in the chain of command.

"Last time we danced it was *Lieutenant* Schaefer," Dillon added, joking, sensing the tension and trying to ease it.

A grin broke out across Schaefer's chiseled face. "Dillon, you son of a bitch," he grumbled good-naturedly. But even though he appeared to lighten up, he filed a red flag on Dillon. At the same time he knew he had no choice but to work with the man, and it was best to make a show of cooperation. Dillon grinned back.

Then the two men simultaneously swung their arms from the hip as if to land a punch. Phillips tensed. But the hands slapped together sharply in a gesture of camaraderie and gamesmanship—massive forearms bulging, testing each other's strength.

"How you been, Dutch?" Dillon inquired, his smile drawn tight only inches form Schaefer's face. He was pushing hard, keeping up the pressure, as if to prove his desk duty hadn't softened him. But Schaefer had the edge from the first, and slowly, methodically, taking his sweet time, he forced Dillon's arm down three or four inches.

"You been sharpening too many pencils, Dillon," said Schaefer, a teasing glint in his eyes. Neither man grunted or even breathed hard. "Had enough?"

"No way, old buddy," Dillon replied through gritted teeth, still cocky, as if to say he was just getting ready to hit the field.

"You never did know when to quit."

The two arms quivered and strained. Dillon's fell another inch. Then a long moment of stasis as the two looked into each other's eyes, each seeming to remember something from the past. Neither blinked. Then they suddenly broke away as if to call it a draw, Schaefer punching Dillon on the shoulder.

"That was some piece of work you guys pulled off in Berlin," said Dillon smoothly, as if there had been no break since the two men greeted each other. Dillon turned slightly so as to include General Phillips. "Sudanese embassy, three weeks ago. They blew the entry points on three floors and neutralized seven terrorists in ten seconds flat. Terrorists didn't even have time to call in their demands. Never made the fuckin' news at all."

"Like the old days, huh, Dillon?" Schaefer replied, not sorry for the recognition in front of his superior officer. Anything to give him more freedom of movement. "Like the man says, no news is good news."

"Yeah. We also heard you passed on that little job in Libya," Dillon added.

Schaefer studied the man who'd left his Washington office to return to the jungle, his eyes narrowing again. "Wasn't my style," he explained curtly as if giving Dillon a brief lesson in protocol. "We're a rescue unit." He smiled. "Like the fuckin' Red Cross. Besides, you got all the assassins you need at Langley, don't you?"

"So they say."

Schaefer turned to the general, who was following them back and forth like a racquetball game, not sure exactly how to break in.

"This must be good," Schaefer said. "Big shot from the CIA splits from his paneled walls to come back to the bush. Has to leave his nice little pork chop secretary, prob'ly dickin' her on the side. So what's so important?"

"Those cabinet members are crucial to our scope of operations in this part of the world," Dillon explained carefully.

"How much you payin' em?" asked Schaefer. "Couple hundred grand a year? They make more than the fuckin' President, don't they?"

Dillon ignored the taunt. He went on gravely. "The point is, they're about to get squeezed. We can't let that happen. I need someone who can get in and get out, quick and quiet—no screwups," he emphasized. "I need the *best*. So I pulled a few strings at State and here we are." There was a certain edge of a boast in his voice, or was it perhaps a dare?

"Go on," Schaefer nodded.

Dillon walked to the wall map. "The setup is simple, Dutch," he said. "One-day job. We pick up their trail at the chopper, run 'em down, grab the hostages, and bounce back over the border before anyone knows we were there. You've done it a hundred times. Nothing out of the ordinary," he stressed. "You and your men can have a nice three-day weekend after. Tie one on in Mexico City. On *us*," he added with a thin smile.

Schaefer thought a minute, studying the strangely featureless map, the wide dense green shot through with a dozen rivers. "And nothing we can't handle alone," he said pointedly, still bristling at the thought of combining his unit with anybody.

Phillips, who'd been standing to the side observing silently, took the opportunity to intercede. "I'm afraid those are your orders, Major," he said evenly to Schaefer. His air of formality was as thick as a huddle of diplomats. "Once you reach your objective, Colonel Dillon will evaluate the situation and take charge."

Schaefer, looking coolly from one to the other, clearly didn't like the arrangement, not even a little bit.

Dillon endeavored once more to smooth the tension. "Not to worry, Dutch," he said calmly. "Hey, I haven't lost my edge. They've got a head start on us in some real tough country, but otherwise, pardner, it's a piece of cake."

Phillips stepped in again, abrupt as a referee, impatient to move the operation along. "Gentlemen, we're losing time," he said, speaking from his rank.

"That's okay, sir," Schaefer replied. "I been working overtime as long as I can remember."

Phillips went on as if he hadn't heard. "You'd better get your men ready now." Then, pausing a moment as if for effect, he added, "Good luck, Major."

Schaefer grinned. "Luck's got nothin' to do with it, General. I gave up luck in high school. I prefer a little deadly force myself."

He saluted and turned and strode out of the hut, Dillon following close at his heels. The general did not look quite so relieved.

TWO

"REDBIRD TWO TWO. Bearing south, three-five-zero, one o'clock on the saddle ridge. Over."

The pilot of one of the assault choppers was shouting into the radio to his brother pilot about a mile and a half behind. They were sailing through a winding canyon, zigzagging up a stream to the site of the crippled craft. Half a moon lit up the barest contours of the jungle terrain, silvering the stream, but there wasn't a single human light anywhere out here. The canyon ended at a sheer cliff with a stream spilling down, and the two choppers rose up and over like drunken birds, leveling off, now racing just above the treetops.

Schaefer studied the rainforest whipping by below, noting how the tangled jungle would suddenly drop off into treacherous canyons and stream beds gorged with watershed, churning up rapids and undermining the massy roots of the rubber trees. Following a ridge he caught a glimpse of a partially exposed Mayan ruin, overgrown with the relentless jungle, its crumbling temple steps reaching for the sky as if to offer one last sacrifice. Altogether a raw and primal place—chaotic, untouched, unyielding—yet Schaefer seemed to take it all in impassively. He'd been through chaos before. There was something almost casual about him, as if he was shrugging his shoulders at the wildness unfurling beneath. The hooded look of his eyes seemed to say: *So what else is new?*

"Roger, Redbird," sputtered a voice through the radio. "Three-five-zero, on your move. Over."

The Redbird pilot confirmed the coordinates as the two craft raced the night, perfectly synchronized, as if they were guided by one central control.

Ten feet away in the belly of the chopper squatted five men dressed in jungle camouflage, black grease streaked across their faces like Aztec warriors. Though nobody talked, nobody was resting. They were methodically checking their weapons, making last-minute adjustments to their gear. Each had been selected for his expertise in a specialized area of combat, and each man knew he was on his own for the doublecheck. You had to pick up your own slack. You got blown up by your own mistakes.

The hull of the craft reverberated with the roar of the engines and the blades spinning above. A little air blew in from the cockpit, but it was close in here like a guerrilla prison, without an inch to maneuver in. The men sat knee to knee, tensed like a brace of caged tigers.

The biggest of the five, Blain Cooper, looked like two hundred and forty pounds of human warhead. Tattooed up and down both arms, a mean five-inch scar across his thick forehead, Cooper was acting as weapons and ordinance specialist for the mission. He removed a thick plug of tobacco from his shirt pocket and gazed across the cabin at Mac Eliot, who was equally huge if a bit cleaner, his large head sitting squarely on his freight-car shoulders, looking as if he had no neck. He held his baby, an M-60 machine gun, cradled in his arms. Blain offered Mac a chew of tobacco, but the latter declined with a slow shake of his head.

They were all set to replay a game they went through at least once a day. Blain loved to perform and needle the rest of them. Holding the plug between teeth stained snot-yellow with years of sucking the vile stuff, he reached across his chest and yanked free a ten-inch combat knife from his shoulder scabbard. Placing the razor sharp blade next to his lips, he sliced through the plug as if it were butter. Then he slurped it into the side of his mouth and chewed thoughtfully.

Sitting beside Blain next to the doorway into the cockpit was Jorge Ramirez, a headstrong, agitated Chicano troublemaker from the Houston barrio. He was all absorbed just now in adding a final piece of camouflage tape to his pack harness. Ramirez was fanatic about details. When at last he'd gotten the tape exactly right, he looked up and smiled. Faking a throw he bulleted the tape to Rick Hawkins, the operations radioman and medic. Hawkins, a freckled and blue-eyed Irish kid from South Boston, was lost in a beat-up copy of *Hustler,* disconnected as a rush-hour commuter. But always alert, he snagged the tape as it flew by with an instinctive snap of the wrist, continuing to read for a moment before looking up.

He grinned at Ramirez; they always made a point of testing each other's reflexes before battle. Hawkins's impish, eager face belied the rugged professional soldier who never thought twice about his own skin. He had saved the ass of every man in the circle at least once.

Ramirez called him "Puddytat" for the nine lives that Hawkins had squeaked through, all the near misses and reckless escapes. Hawkins was the team's lucky charm.

Next to Hawkins sat Billy Sole, the Kit Carson scout. His shiny coal-black hair was two inches longer than regulation, which went to show what regulations Major Schaefer put his money on. Billy was half Sioux and half Italian, and his two natures maintained a hostile peace, like a dog and a cat tied up at the same stake. He was lean and incredibly fast, but he sat against the bulkhead now with total poise as he quietly replaced the firing mechanism of his M-203, repeatedly testing its action. The steady click of the hammer seemed to have a hypnotic effect on him, but you didn't want to move too quick when Billy was around. Even when he was relaxed he was like a snake under a rock.

Hawkins moved to stir Billy's calm demeanor. "Hey, Billy, how many marines does it take to eat a squirrel?" Billy gave him a blank unblinking stare. Hawkins quickly added: "Two. One to eat it and one to watch for cars." He guffawed heartily at his own joke.

As the men prepped for the mission at hand—which they all knew could amount to anything from a quick pickup to a bloody battle—the helicopters cleared another high ridge and plunged into a steep descent, turning sharply into a deep-walled canyon. The cabin tilted suddenly, and the screaming turbines shifted into a lower key. The men in the circle pitched forward with the motion, but restraining harnesses kept them in place, even though they were nearly upside down as the chopper made the radical descent.

When they were righted again Blain held out the plug of tobacco to Ramirez, who swatted at the offensive object as if it were alive.

"Get that stinkin' thing outa my face, Blain!"

Grinning now from ear to ear Blain made the rounds, offering the plug to each man. All refused ritualistically. They'd been through this a hundred times. Nobody took any real offense. It was a reassuring dose of reality and a sign of how closely they knew one another. In the rituals lay their bonding and mutual respect, the kind of tightness that developed from spotting each other in the teeth of death. Their honor was all bound up in being united. They had no friends or brothers back home. To all intents and purposes there *was* no back home. They were only alive in action, and they needed one another the way they needed guns.

"Bunch of slack-jawed faggots." Blain feigned disgust as he spat between his legs. "This stuff'll put hair on your hogleg," he bragged, waving the sticky plug to make his point. "It'll make you a goddam sexual ty-ran-toe-sore-ass just like me!" And he howled as loud as the engine while the others clapped and booed and whistled.

The chopper made another sharp turn. Up in the cockpit the agenda was a little more focused. Schaefer and Dillon, headsets linked to the pilot's, were poring over an infrared map with pencil lights.

Dillon pointed to the northwest quadrant. "Rendezvous points and radio frequencies indicated and fixed," he said. "AWACS contact on four-hour intervals. Signal hasn't changed since the craft went down. We can't figure why the guerrillas didn't just smash the radio."

"Who's backup on this?" Schaefer asked.

Dillon shook his head. "Doesn't exist on this one, old buddy," Dillon replied. "Once we cross that border we're on our own."

"I don't mean backup *here*," retorted Schaefer disdainfully, as if any added support would be a show of weakness. "I'm talkin' backup *there*," he said, reaching over to nudge Dillon's briefcase. The briefcase seemed to represent all of Washington, from the Pentagon to the White House.

"Negative," Dillon replied. "Nobody knows we're here. Nobody wants to know."

"This gets better by the minute," Schaefer said slyly, eyes brightening perceptibly in the glinting light of his pencil flash. Nothing Dutch Schaefer liked better than everyone acting like he didn't exist.

The pilots of the two helicopters were communicating their point positions: "Roger Bird Double Two. Reconfirm insertion at Tango, Charlie, Delta one-zero, niner on the grid at zero-two-two, mark four by zero. Over."

The string of numbers coursed through the static like an alien tongue. The Redbird cockpit began to pulse with a green glow as the stabilizer gauge was activated to the landing mode.

In front of the pilot was a radar sweep and an infrared display terminal on which the two helicopters appeared as heat sources, yellow on a gray ground. At about four o'clock on the terminal appeared a third lozenge of yellow, dimmer than the others and not moving. The downed chopper was east/southeast, somewhere in a five-mile quadrant. It was impossible to pin down any closer, since the terrain was so steep and thickly covered. The team would just have to be dropped so they could close in on it at ground level.

The coordinates confirmed, the pilot announced a landing time of two minutes. Then he threw a switch on the panel just beside the steering column, and a blue light flashed on the chopper's nose, another by the for-

ward bulkhead. The pilot turned and handed Dillon a
clipboard with the landing numbers penciled in, re-
questing approval. Dillon nodded, initialing the landing
plan as fastidiously as if he were sitting at his desk at
Langley.

Blue light flared over the thick jungle, the black wall
of night swallowing it as it combed the tangled trees.
The support helicopter held almost motionless in a protective position above Redbird. It had been obvious for
some time that they weren't going to find a clearing to
touch down in. The men were going to have to rappel
down cables. The best the pilot could do was find a
patch of undergrowth that would keep them free of the
trees.

As the blue light revealed a likely target ground beside a stream the two pilots began to maneuver into
position. Dillon stood up and made his way past the
forward bulkhead and entered the belly where the five
men hunkered in a circle. He held up both thumbs to
give them the signal to get prepared, but nobody moved
right away. They didn't need a full two minutes to evac-
uate a craft. The whole team could explode out of there
in fifteen seconds flat. There seemed to be a point of
pride in showing Dillon how they did things their way.
Unstated of course, perhaps not even conscious, but
these guys were always proving something. You didn't
drink a pint of whiskey if somebody else was packing
away a fifth.

In any case, Dillon was keenly aware of his outsider
status. He stood in the doorway uneasily, aware that the
men were watching him, mostly without expression.
Absently Dillon pulled from his pocket a battered cigarette lighter. On it was the crest of the snarling panther,

emblem of the famed commando unit he'd served in in
Thailand with Schaefer. Casually he held it out to show
it to Ramirez, who was closest to him.

But the gesture didn't work, perhaps because the
Redbird team didn't give two shits about the Army, past
or present. Dillon's attempt to share a personal moment
came across as merely self-serving, and Ramirez and
the others knew it. The Chicano bent closer over his
pack harness, leaving the black man in the lurch. Dillon
simply had to accept the fact that they saw him as a desk
man and an opportunist who couldn't hide his status in
those starched fatigues.

Mac, observing this interchange, looked over at his
buddy Blain, his beady eyes narrowing as he nodded in
Dillon's direction. Blain continued to roll his jaw, mas-
ticating the tobacco. He paused, eyes on the floor, then
hocked a thick vile stream of juice directly between Dillon's legs and onto the floor of the cabin. A thin gela-
tinous skein of the stuff laced across the toe of one of
Dillon's combat boots.

Dillon looked up, his face stone cold and menacing.
"Man, that's a real bad habit you got," he said icily. He
didn't seem quite so unsure of himself now. If they were
going to play hard to get, well, two could play that
game too.

Dillon turned back into the cockpit as Mac and Blain
grinned at each other in triumph. They'd just won a
small guerrilla skirmish, further confirming their opin-
ion of Dillon as a spineless character. To these guys at
least, Dillon couldn't win for losing; he had Washington, D.C., written all over him. The five commandos
were active-duty lifers. They even disdained R and R,
unless it was a three-day drunk. To them Dillon was a

pussy and a cop-out till he proved otherwise.

A moment later the pilot's voice broke in over Schaefer's headset. "LZ comin' up thirty degrees," he announced. "Stand by the rappel lines."

Schaefer, acknowledging the message with a hand signal, leaned back and ducked his head through the doorway, nodding to his men. They sprang into action, as if to acknowledge the presence of their *real* commanding officer. Ramirez and Blain gathered up the landing gear, four steel conical devices hooked to canvas bags filled with coils of rope. Hawkins stationed himself at the door and tossed them out, the lines hurling through the air, crashing through thick layers of underbrush and slamming into the jungle floor below.

As the landing proceeded to active the blue light changed to green, signaling the go-ahead for disembarking. Mac shouted to Hawkins: "What's it look like down there, Irish?"

"Pile o' dogshit!"

"Hey, fabulous! Next stop, Beverly Hills!"

They all stood up and pushed forward like they were coming out of a huddle, nudging one another as they moved toward the door, grunting with anticipation. They were not the kind of men who crossed themselves before they jumped.

Mac went first, then Blain, scrambling onto the ropes with gloved hands. They disappeared together down into the darkness, Blain sending up a hoot like he was riding a bucking bronc.

Next Billy, then Ramirez. Hawkins held back as Schaefer and Dillon pulled off their headsets and came back from the cockpit. Schaefer nodded to Hawkins to go ahead, and the Irishman pulled on his gloves, grabbed the cable, and swung out the door and down. There was the slightest pause as Dillon and Schaefer stepped to the doorway. Schaefer normally bailed out last, but here again the protocol intervened. Dillon knew Dutch Schaefer too well not to know how it galled him to yield to a higher rank, especially in the field. Schaefer was a great commando and a lousy soldier. But he betrayed no ruffled feelings as he drew on his gloves and reached for the cable.

"Wait a minute, Dutch," said Dillon, and the blond man paused in the doorway, the big muscles in his shoulders rippling with tension. "I think the man said we gotta get there first. Then I can start fuckin' up."

And with a grin he moved past Schaefer and gripped the cable and bulleted out the door. Dutch was clearly startled by the show of respect—and just as clearly pleased. Lunging out into the wet night air himself, with the engine shrieking three feet from his ear, he started to think maybe Dillon hadn't turned completely flab after all.

"You don't know how much I missed this, pal!" Dillon exclaimed as the two men swung down the twin cables. "Once you get it in your blood, you're hooked!"

Schaefer shouted back: "Man, you been readin' too many Marvel comics!"

As the two of them dropped to the jungle floor they hunched up, crashing through a tangle of ferns and elephant leaves, then thumping the earth as their heavy boots dug into the spongy ground. As soon as they let go of the cables the automatic winch in the chopper began to reel in the lines.

Redbird didn't waste a second. It whapped away into the darkness, its brother chopper following. Suddenly the soldiers were severed from their airborne lifeline, alone in the wildness of the jungle, their bridge to safety disappearing like a rumble of distant thunder.

THREE

THE PREDAWN SKY was streaked in the east with mackerel clouds. The zing of insects and the rush of water in the swollen stream were deafening. As the seven men gathered their gear they began to distinguish the outlines of towering rubber trees. A light shower had left a glistening veneer of fine mist on the lush foliage and a slick humid edge to the air. Even as the mosquitoes hummed around their heads the first morning birds began to trill, signaling the start of the day's chorus. It would shortly become a cacaphony of clicking, warbling, and screeching as everything from hummingbirds to prowling cats let loose their shimmer of sound effects through the course of the tropical day.

As the sky turned pearl and then pale rose the temperature began to inch up as if the jungle were having a fever dream about the midday heat. Slowly the sky broke clear as the first pulse of the sun evaporated the cloak of mist on the landscape. The commandos loaded their packs on their backs, surveying their surroundings cautiously, peering close at the seemingly limitless screen of jungle.

Triggered by a command from Schaefer the team

began to move out, the pace set medium-brutal by Ramirez as pointman. They were synchronized perfectly about fifteen feet apart, each man carrying eighty or ninety pounds as they headed into the trees. It was mostly weapons and ammo. On a mission like this they didn't eat except what they could scavenge in the field, and they didn't need tents because they wouldn't be sleeping. Everything extraneous had been eliminated from their gear. There wasn't a toothbrush among them.

Well, maybe Dillon had a toothbrush.

As they came through the rubber trees and started downhill they encountered an even denser growth of jungle, so thick the seven were visually parted most of the time, though they held to a strict five meters between. Their highly tuned instincts and combat expertise kept them moving in unison, beginning now to work up a heavy sweat. The only sound of their progress was Ramirez hacking away up ahead with his machete, lopping off bush leaves and breaking vines. Otherwise they moved like prowlers, creeping down the makeshift trail, not letting so much as a twig crack.

After half an hour of arduous downhill hiking, Schaefer stopped for a compass check. Then he whistled a signal to Ramirez—one long and two short—to set a new direction, west/southwest. As they resumed marching the slope leveled out and they found themselves in a marshy area, slogging through mud to their ankles, smacking at black flies that left their arms and necks bloody. It was nearly an hour before they reached solid ground again, with tree ferns waving over their heads and a smell like ripe peaches.

At last they broke through into a clearing. Blain went up to the head of the column and crouched in a defen-

sive position, scanning the area with his MP-5 at the
ready. About a hundred yards away in a circle of stony
ground he spotted the wreckage of the army UH-1H
chopper. It was hanging upside down, wedged in an
enormous stand of century cactus ten feet above the
ground. The rotors were bent and twisted, the canopy
mangled badly, and the tail section completely severed,
thrown clear of the wreck and on the ground, fifteen
feet from the nest of cactus. Except for the distant grate
of parrots the setting was quiet, as after a bomb.

Cautiously they approached the gnarled tail, collapsed like a fallen kite, the metal burned to ash as thin
as paper. At an order from Schaefer, Mac moved forward into the shadow of the cactus. It was more like a
grove than a single plant, its myriad spiked arms shooting as high as thirty feet, as if spurred by some genetic
flaw that ran rampant through the jungle terrain. Now
and then out here a thing got so gigantic it grew unearthly—an orchid, a grasshopper, sometimes a frog.
The dead chopper lay in the twisted arms of the cactus
like a fly in a Venus trap.

Playing loops of sturdy rope lightly over one hand,
Mac hurled up a grappling hook and snagged the chopper's cargo hold. The hook went *thunk* and quavered
along the bare metal of the cabin. Ramirez shinnied up
the rope quick as a monkey and cautiously ran his knife
around the chopper's doorway, inspecting for trip wires.
Then, satisfied that the wreck hadn't been booby-
trapped by the guerrillas, he pulled himself over the
edge of the shattered door. Facing him were two bodies,
pilot and co-pilot, dangling upside down and still
strapped into their seats, arms above their heads as if
surrendering. Ramirez didn't blink. Methodically he

glanced around, visually inspecting every square inch of the cabin, then rappeled back down the rope to the ground.

Meanwhile, Dillon had secured a second line and gone up. He was the only one authorized to go through the dead men's uniforms, and he'd been instructed to take out all flight plans and records.

"The pilots each got one round in the head," Ramirez told Schaefer. "And whoever hit it stripped the shit out of it."

Schaefer, his eyes constantly darting around the clearing, turned and looked up at the chopper. A curl of distaste was on his lips.

"Took 'em out with a heat seeker," he said tightly.

"There's something else, Major," Ramirez added quietly.

"What's that?"

"I don't think she's no ordinary army taxi."

Schaefer looked at the younger soldier, his gaze level and slightly quizzical, as if to dare Ramirez to hit him with something unpleasant.

"Looks more like a surveillance bird to me," sniffed Ramirez, nodding slightly, a trifle cocky.

Just then, Dillon came hurtling back to the ground and strode over to Schaefer and Ramirez. *Oh, Jesus,* thought Schaefer, *he's got a real bug up his ass now.*

"You picked up their trail yet?" Dillon asked curtly.

"Billy's on it," Schaefer replied, motioning Ramirez away so he could talk to Dillon privately. Pointing up at the chopper, he drawled, "Heat seeker. Pretty sophisticated for half-ass mountain boys, don't you think?" He smiled thinly. "They're getting better equipped every day. Thank you, Miss America."

But Schaefer was more puzzled than he showed. He was startled at the level of technology the rebel forces had managed to obtain. A gnawing sense that something was "off" began to creep between his shoulders as Billy came trotting across the clearing.

"Major, looks like there were ten, maybe twelve guerrillas. They pulled some prisoners from the chopper," he said, pointing to a set of tracks nearby. Then, with an odd turn in his voice: "I don't know what them other tracks are."

"What other tracks?"

" 'Bout six of 'em, I think," Billy replied carefully. "U.S.-issue jungle boots. They come in from the north, out of them bushes, then they seem to follow the guerrillas. I don't know . . ."

Schaefer, more confused with every detail, turned to Dillon brusquely. "Mean anything to you?" he asked, just short of an accusation.

"Probably another rebel patrol," said Dillon with a shrug. "They operate in here all the time. The whole fuckin' country's crawlin' with 'em."

"It's the weirdest thing," Billy said softly, half to himself.

Schaefer shot him a look. "What is?"

"Those tracks from the north. It's like . . ." Billy seemed to be at a total loss for words. He knew tracks like a bloodhound. "It's like all these six guys have the same size shoes. And they all weigh . . . about one sixty. Every print is perfect." He shook his head, bewildered, as if he couldn't understand himself what he was trying to say. "They march like a fuckin' machine," he added lamely.

"Go up ahead," said Schaefer, cutting him off, impatient with the vagueness. "See what you can find."

Ramirez trotted after Billy as the latter crossed the clearing, eyes to the ground and sifting every inch. From his Sioux ancestors Billy had hawk's eyes, hooded and black and very old. He could probably pick up an ant's tracks.

As if to put Dillon on notice for the next phase of the mission, Schaefer turned to his commanding officer and spoke precisely: "We don't want any accidents. Sir."

By now it was eight in the morning and felt like noon. The heat seemed to grab a man by the throat, hanging on for the kill like a razorback. Grimly, without another word, the two men joined the others. Then they all pushed ahead, lumbering like dinosaurs under the weight of their heavy gear, following the trail Ramirez carved out of the dense undergrowth.

About twenty yards north of the clearing a red and ochre spotted butterfly flew in among the prickly vines that hung like high-tension wires from the gray-barked cottonwood trees. Randomly, as if it needed to pause to get its bearings, the vivid creature landed on a cottonwood branch, still flexing its wings lightly even at rest, its feet hardly touching the gnarled bark. A moment later the insect flew off, leaving a curious imprint on the bark like a shadow of itself, almost like an X-ray.

Up close in fact, the bark didn't look like wood matter at all. It seemed made up of microscopic scales, as if this one tree were fashioned out of some kind of synthetic. Then the printed shadow of the butterfly seemed to bleed into the bark itself, and finally the image disappeared, swallowed into the tree. The branch was moving slightly now, but not as if rustled by any breeze. It almost appeared to be breathing. Then it quivered and began to withdraw toward the trunk of the tree, silent as a boa constrictor.

Now what had seemed to be just another cottonwood tree began to ripple with color, iridescent as a chameleon. Some weird flow of force was making its way through the molecules of the tree, groping toward the roots. For all anyone knew, this sort of transformation happened all the time in the Usamacinta jungle. Perhaps it was only more of the same force that grew the six-inch orchids and the grasshoppers big as mice.

For all anyone knew, that is. But no one knew. No one had even the first glimmering of an idea.

For the tree creature breathed the jungle differently from those who had evolved there. In reality it was no more a cottonwood branch than it was anything else on earth. It somehow discerned living tissue from inanimate objects by picking up the heat patterns of living cells. It saw the outlines of all living creatures shaded with a sort of liquid color that was the pulse of the heat of life. But "saw" is very imprecise, for it only had eyes when it felt like having eyes. It was like a lost soul searching for a form in which to flower. And now suddenly it had focused its yearnings on the most developed creature in the world it had come to visit—man.

As the team struggled through the brush, the creature followed them like an obsession beneath the jungle floor, rippling from root to root. It drove forward like a mad scientist consumed by his own curiosity. It still required a thousand clues to what made a man tick. Since it needed no earthly form of its own beyond what it chose to assume, it was incapable of feeling emotion toward any of the earthling tribes. It knew no pity and no remorse. It was the war and the warrior all in one.

* * *

It was the sweltering height of day now, and the jungle was blaring with the white noise of insects and birds, all the raw life in the rough terrain screaming without reason.

Schaefer by now had consulted his map and compass and outlined another change in course. He passed a hand signal down the line—voices might alert the guerrillas—and the group followed him obediently. Dillon, for all his seniority, was content to let Dutch do the navigating. His own inner compass was rusty, and he knew it.

About an hour later the team broke through a screen of black-leaf palmetto and hit up at the base of a hillside, deeply grooved by the porous volcanic rock and veiled with tree ferns more suited to the higher altitude than the ground-hugging tangle that grew in the heat-trapped valley. A hundred yards up they could see Ramirez standing on a boulder, scouting the valley. He signaled down to the cluster of men that he sighted nothing and they should come ahead.

Billy had left Ramirez and climbed down into a wide crevasse, following the slope of the hill in a gradual curve. He kept stepping on frogs, and twice he had to squeeze through narrow openings in the eroded black rock. Within a couple of minutes he couldn't hear Ramirez whistle from the perch behind him, because his own breath came so heavy in the steep-walled passage.

He stopped for a moment, his mouth and throat parched. He looked up and singled out a curling vine with tiny orange blossoms. He pulled his knife from his shoulder scabbard as he yanked the vine down from its grip on the rock wall and severed its midsection. A thin stream of yellow fluid leaked out, and he sucked it into his thirsty gullet.

Suddenly, alerted to the sense of a suspicious presence, he dropped the vine aside and the yellow liquor trickled out over the ground. He brought his M-203 to attention, aiming it along the tunnel of the crevasse to where it turned a blind corner. His instincts told him something was wrong. He strained his eyes to penetrate the dense canopy of tangled vines and leaves above him, searching for a sign.

It wasn't a sighting, or even a sound that alerted him. In his thirteen years of combat duty he'd learned to freeze at any sudden change in his field of focus, even when there was no identifiable evidence. Billy was possessed of a keen sixth sense, and his hunches were seldom wrong. In the wild, faced with the possibility of encountering an enemy who would kill you as easily as swat a fly, you never ignored even faint, unconfirmed warnings. Sometimes Billy would find himself overcome with an aura of death. As soon as you felt it you had to be ready to kill. There was no second shot in the jungle.

Complicating Billy's perceptions were the deafening sounds of the midday scree of wildlife. The clicks and buzzings, the cries of tropical birds and the gabble of monkeys, all were magnified a hundredfold by the relentless heat. Even down here in the dark tunnel there wasn't a breath of cool. It was like being in a pressure cooker about to burst.

Realizing there was nothing immediate, Billy relaxed slightly and began to move again, the two rock walls on either side barely as wide as his shoulders. He came to the blind corner and peered around it, startled to see the crevasse open out to the hillside. He felt a rush of relief as he stepped away from the cavelike recess, feeling again the beat of the sun on his neck.

Still he couldn't see ten feet ahead through the ferns, and as he started across the slope he forced himself to be totally alert, paying special attention to the new terrain. He couldn't put his finger on it, but he wasn't at all satisfied that nothing beyond the natural interplay of the jungle was at work. There was something out there ticking, even if he couldn't hear it yet.

A few minutes later Billy crouched and stared at the ground in front of him. He looked confused as he traced a bootprint in the mud, then another. He looked up and combed the trees with his keen eyes, ears perked for any sound that didn't fit in the flow of things. What was it, he wondered, about these bootprints? Why did they seem too perfect?

Hearing a faint rustling, he sprang to his feet. He moved forward through the ferns, finger on the double trigger of his gun. Ahead he could see a heavy curtain of moss hanging among the trees. As he got closer he saw the moss was swarming with hundreds of flies buzzing like a chainsaw. Had that been the sound that was out of synch? Cautiously he stepped forward, cutting a spider web out of his path with the barrel of his cocked gun. A queer smell made his nostrils flare, but he wasn't thinking absolutely clearly all of a sudden. His mind seemed to skip a beat, as if he thought for a moment he was back in Louisiana, hunting coon with his brother.

Reaching forward, Billy touched the slick tendrils of moss with his free hand. He saw something rustling behind the curtain and a weird shifting of dark forms. He shuddered slightly as he stared at his hand where it stroked the trailing tree moss. Then, holding his breath, with a swift movement of his gloved hand he swept the moss aside.

Instantly an explosion of fluttering black wings blinded him as vultures erupted in ten directions. They shrieked past Billy, enraged at his intrusion, wingtips and claws batting him about the face and arms as he stood there stunned. Their blood cry churned his belly like an old Sioux war call.

Then, as the black cloud of carrion scavengers disappeared, Billy's face froze into a mask of horror. His eyes bulged and his mouth went slack as he fell into a state of raw shock. A curl of disgust gurgled in his throat as he stared transfixed at the horror inches from his ancient eyes.

It was the leering death-grin of a human face completely stripped of skin, glistening with newly exposed muscle tissue and dripping with blood. The body was hanging upside down like a side of beef, every inch of skin methodically flayed, precise as if a team of demented surgeons had been at work. Some muscles still twitched as the body swayed in the humid breeze.

In shock, Billy stumbled backward and lost his footing, then hugged the trunk of a tree and let the vomit come. As he stood quaking in a cold sweat, a little distance now between him and the horrible face, he took in the rest of the gruesome scene. Suspended from branches above, vines threaded through their Achilles tendons, hung the bodies of three dead men. Each was completely gutted and skinned. Thousands of insects beat the air as they attacked the carcasses in a crazed, exultant mass feeding.

Billy—the mercenary who had survived the worst trench wars from Angola to Cambodia—turned away as he felt his throat roar with the urge to scream. He put a hand to his mouth and bit his fingers, gasping for air, controlling the gag reflex, then forced himself to turn away just as Ramirez stepped quietly into view. Schaefer was a couple of paces behind him.

Gaping at the decomposing and desecrated bodies ravaged by the vultures, a whimpering Ramirez crossed himself in an almost childlike way.

"Holy Mother," he gasped, his voice shaking. Then he shouted over his shoulder, breaking the code of silence. "Somebody—somebody get some help!" he cried.

As if he'd forgotten that they were the help. As if he still didn't realize, even with the evidence bleeding all over the matted ground, just how very alone they were.

FOUR

As Billy and Ramirez stood there frozen and helpless, Schaefer moved into the clearing, kneeling beside the bloody pile of clothing and entrails. He examined the discarded gear carefully, turning it over, then stood up holding a dog tag on a broken chain. His expression grew stony, his face taut and strained as he stared at the tag, recognizing the name.

"'J.S. Davis, Captain, U.S. Army,'" he read out loud, toneless and grim. His bewildered eyes moved from the dogtag up to the gutted bodies. He swallowed once, and a muscle in his jaw fluttered for a second. Then he turned and faced the six men who stood pale and dumbstruck at the clearing's edge.

"Cut them down, Mac," he instructed coldly. The evenness of his voice masked a rage beyond a mere soldier's revenge after a bloody battle. Davis and Schaefer had a long history together. Since boot camp nearly twenty years ago, they had been mates and comrades. They'd barely squeaked out with their skins on a secret mission in Malaysia in seventy-nine. Davis was the best chopper pilot in the business, and he'd twice come in under fire to scoop Dutch up. Silently

Schaefer vowed to destroy whoever had desecrated his friend. Now it was private between him and the enemy. He would walk through hell to make them pay.

Mac moved forward, obeying Schaefer's command. He shinnied up the tree and one by one cut the bodies down. With a slice of his razor-edge combat knife, the severed vine released the first corpse, and it fell with a sickly thud to the ground. Then the second, then the third. The men stood around like an honor guard, too proud to fall apart, steeling themselves till the shock had passed, knowing that as with Schaefer it would quickly slide into rage and make them strong again. Mac bent over the bloody pile, picking out the other two dog tags.

At last Schaefer turned to Dillon, who had been standing silently like the others, mouth slightly agape, as incapacitated as the men he was meant to lead.

"I knew this man," said the major, holding the dog tag close to Dillon's face, swaying it like a hypnotist. "Green Beret, out of Fort Bragg. What the hell was he doing in here? Last I heard he was runnin' taxi service to Camp David, transportin' the Big Man's sheepdog. He needed a tour of jungle duty like he needed a second dick. So what's he doin' gettin' himself scalped in this jerkwater two-bit country? You got any answers to that, Dillon?" he demanded angrily.

"It's—it's inhuman, that's what it is," Dillon replied with difficulty. "I'm sorry, Dutch, I didn't know—"

"Maybe we should call the ACLU, huh? See if we can file a little complaint. All nice and typed, ya know?" His voice was thick with contempt.

"Look, Dutch, I wasn't told about any covert operations in this area. They shouldn't have been here. I would have known."

"Well, somebody sent 'em," Schaefer snapped, unsatisfied and irritated. As of this moment he was clearly uninterested in official bullshit. He walked off as Mac stepped out of the clearing, sheathing his knife with a violent gesture as he passed Ramirez.

"Must've run into guerrillas . . . fuckin' animals," growled Ramirez. He wiped his sweaty dirt-encrusted brow with his forearm, then realized his hands were shaking. He shoved them violently into his pockets.

Everyone was trying to understand, to throw together some rational reason how this thing could have happened. None of them had ever seen such barbaric treatment by an enemy—not in Cambodia, not in Lebanon, not in all their combined years of combat service, which probably amounted to a century. Deep down they still believed that between enemies there was an unwritten code, setting limits to the degree of torture inflicted, at least among so-called professional soldiers. This was so far beyond the code that they didn't even have any context for it. Why strip a man of his skin? Why bother? There were so many easier ways to hurt. It was like some demented autopsy.

"Ain't no way for a soldier to die," Mac said tightly to Blain, hawking a yellow-brown stream of chew saliva that landed on a banana flower, drooling to the ground. "Time to get ol' painless out," he added with relish. He ripped at the Velcro closures on the canvas bag draped over his shoulder and pulled out his baby: a six-barreled automatic adapted for field combat. It caught the sun's rays and glimmered darkly, deadly as a portable minefield.

Billy had meanwhile moved a short distance ahead of the others and was examining the ground beyond the carnage. He plucked at the beaten grass several times, as if he were picking up coins. Then he stood and held out for Schaefer to see a handful of spent cartridges. Dutch walked over to him.

"What happened here, Billy?" he asked quietly, sensing the younger man's churning mind as he desperately struggled to put it together. Schaefer knew well that of all his men, Billy had the most intuitive feel for unraveling a puzzle. Billy moved to a subtler rhythm, his ears tuned to a higher pitch. Schaefer used to tell him he was part bird dog, part witch doctor.

"I don't get it, Major," Billy said haltingly. Yet as always he was stubbornly certain, no matter how mismatched the evidence seemed. "There was a firefight here. Shooting in all directions. Like four, five hundred rounds."

"I can't believe Jack Davis walked straight into an ambush, even if he *was* a prisoner," Schaefer retorted, recalling his dead friend's radar. Davis had eyes at the back of his head. Nothing had ever taken him by surprise. In that he was just like Schaefer himself. The whole idea of an ambush was an insult.

"No, it wasn't like that, sir," Billy agreed. "Besides, there's not a single track to show what they were shooting *at*. It's like they were firing like crazy into the air. It just doesn't make sense." Billy scratched the stubble on his chin and brooded a moment. "And I don't know *where* the fuck those guys with the new boots went. They must have turned off somewhere."

"Wait a minute—what about the rest of Jack's men?" Schaefer was vehement. It was as if he wanted to slap Billy back to reality—whatever that was. "Where're the guerrillas who took 'em out of the chopper? And where're the goddam politicians?" He was practically yelling now.

Billy shook his head. "No sign," he said simply. "They never left here, Major." Then, shying at the mystery of it even as he told it, he added awkwardly: "It's like they kind of disappeared."

Schaefer struggled a moment, grappling to form a strategy in his head. Then, with a huge effort of will, he instructed bluntly: "Find me a trail, Billy. I wanna blow me away some guerrillas."

Turning to the rest of the team he barked: "Okay guys, funeral's over. Let's keep movin'. Five-meter spread. Don't even breathe."

Like lightning the major had thrown all systems to full throttle, which in his case was several cylinders more explosive than an eighteen-wheeler. But he simply couldn't endure ambiguity and inaction. It was as if his muscles and mind together suddenly snapped to attention, senses cued for anything and everything. His veins pumped with adrenalin as he whipped himself up to combat mode—all engine, power on—into a force of near superhuman prowess.

The others quickly geared up, too, following Schaefer like a coach. Though none could match his uncanny stamina or his brute singlemindedness, at least they could keep pace with him. Psyching themselves for an encounter with whoever was responsible for the senseless torture and desecration, the men readied themselves for battle each in his own way.

Blain fed a magazine of belted shells into his weapon, cocking it till it ached to shoot. He looked up at Mac as he loaded. Mac retied his boots with total absorption, stringing them up and pulling them tight as

if the exact tension mattered—he would live or die by
the lacing of his boots. Dillon jotted a compass reading
in his notebook. Ramirez absentmindedly polished his
black pearl ring on the sleeve of his fatigues. Hawkins
adjusted the pins on two grenades and clipped them onto
his belt; then drew out a comb and eased it through his
black Irish hair.

But at some moment in the elaborate ritual, each
managed to exchange half a second's glance with the
others. They acknowledged their camaraderie obliquely,
but somehow understanding the mix of signals in one
another's eyes—the anger, the fear, the lifeblood support. And twined through it all like the grip of a vine in
a cottonwood tree was the certainty of death—their
mates', their enemy's, their own. A match had been lit
deep in the mine, and the fuel that would feed the fire
might turn out to be the whole dark earth itself.

"Payback time," Blain declared with controlled rage
as he hefted the gun and poised the butt of it on his hip.
Mac drew back on the breech bolt of his M-60, letting it
snap into fire position. They grinned at each other,
ready to find and face gooks, Huns, and Tartars.

The blood-warrior hue of their faces streaked with
camouflage grease was in strange contrast to their high-
tech combat gear. It was like Hannibal crossing the Alps
with V-1 rockets on the elephants' backs. Mac and
Blain, heading out in tandem, urged each other forward,
a constant dare playing between them. That, and the
memory of the brutal murders they'd just discovered,
made them hungry to shoot first and ask no questions at
all. If somebody innocent got in the way, so be it. Mac
and Blain didn't get all misty-eyed about innocence.
Just as well not to ask them their opinions about My
Lai.

And observing them from the highest branches of a densely leafed baobab tree, the invader didn't miss a beat. Incapable of guilt or rage or fear or pity, unable to understand that what it had done to the dead was a vile dishonor, it absorbed the marching commandos through its heat-sensitive optic cells. It hid so deep in the tree that it was impossible to say what form it took, whether monkey or crow or something more mutant. If one of the men had looked straight into the leaves with binoculars, he might have caught the yellow gleam of an eye, but the eye was only a nexus of nerves, spun from its own secretions like an insect's nest. Though it stared and took in everything it did not need to see or to comprehend. It had evolved beyond such concepts eons ago. Yet still it could not stop looking.

The men below knew nothing beyond themselves. Each took his own measure and adapted himself to the brutal terrain, blocking out everything but forward movement and absolute silence. Even with his enormous bulk Mac moved gracefully, soundlessly through the jungle. As he stepped along light as a deer, Dillon followed five meters behind. The black man accidentally stepped on the broken branch of a felled tree, his foot crunching through the rotting, grub-infested wood. A chunk broke loose and rolled down the hill, gathering bark and gravel, finally landing at the base of a rock with a *thunk*. Not a lot of noise, but it couldn't have been made by anything else but a man.

At once Dillon cringed and tightened into a defensive posture, listening for any signs that he had given away their position. The jungle was unmoved as he strained his eyes and ears, terrified he'd announced the team's presence to the enemy. Accidents were not permissible under the tense circumstances. Dillon felt like a horse's ass. This never would've happened if he'd only had a couple of days to get himself in shape. Twenty-four hours ago he was sitting dazed at his desk at Langley, being given the sudden orders for this mission. He had a bad ache in his calf muscle, and he'd managed to twist his back tripping over a root. Horse's ass was right.

As Dillon listened, teeth gritted at his own stupidity, Mac appeared silently from behind a bush, parting its broad leaves. He stood within inches of Dillon's face, eyes burning with contempt and anger.

"You're ghostin' on me, mutha' fokaa!" he hissed, spraying spittle in the black man's face. "I don't give a shit what kinda big dick you got in Washington. You give away my position again and I'll bleed you quiet and leave your fuckin' ass right here. And you can write your fuckin' senator if you don't like it. Got it, pal?"

Dillon glared back in cold hatred, but he didn't answer back. He was stalemated by combat rules he knew as well as Mac, and he'd just broken them. Mac turned and vanished into the undergrowth. When his gun was cocked Mac didn't give two squats about the chain of command. Even at the best of times he didn't call anyone "Sir," not even Schaefer.

Dillon was left thrown and speechless, staring at the rustle of leaves that had swallowed Mac. But Dillon didn't have any recourse, official or otherwise. He picked up the trail again, this time watching every footfall.

Meanwhile, Mac had caught up with Blain, who was crouched beneath a banana palm, chewing quietly on a banana, absorbing the texture of his surroundings. He looked more like a gorilla than usual. Mac sidled up to him, and they spoke in whispers.

"Say, Bull. What's goin' down? We got movement?"

"Naw," Mac murmured. "Shithead with the trench-coat was makin' enough racket to get us all waxed. Don't let him get too close behind ya, huh? You don't wanna wind up skinned like a rabbit." He chuckled hoarsely, his voice strained from whispering. Then he wiped his forehead with the back of his hand. Sweat mixed with dust and melting grease was dripping into his eyes, stinging and clouding his vision.

Blain patted his weapon affectionately. "I hear you, Bull," he nodded. "But don't sweat it, man. Me and ol' painless here're watchin' the front door. The nig-nog can play chopsticks on his drums, I don't care."

As stubborn and hardened as these two were, their sense of brotherhood was critical; and they felt a need to remind themselves of it in the face of Dillon's incompetence. They were also thoroughly enjoying Dillon's outsider status, relishing the difficulty the black man was having keeping up the pace. If someone had called them on the racial slurs they would have looked completely blank. Mac and Blain slurred everybody. They didn't spend a lot of their free time going to weddings and christenings.

Mac advanced another ten meters, stuck his head out of the bushes to reconnoiter, then signaled slowly. The rest of the assault team moved swiftly up the hill, barely visible in the dense brush as they dispersed into defensive position. The bushes stopped just at the brow of the hill, which had been slashed and burned to serve as lookout, though no one stood sentry right now. The knoll appeared completely deserted as the commandos took stock and proceeded out of cover, crawling on their bellies across blackened ground alive with scurrying insects.

The top of the knoll was almost peaceful, certainly

quieter than the surrounding jungle, the blue sky brilliant above the tropical afternoon. The men, camouflaged as much by the ash and dirt as by their combat motley, were drenched with sweat as the bare, dark ground absorbed the harsh rays of the equatorial sun, increasing the temperature just above the turf to a searing hundred and ten degrees.

Schaefer and Ramirez were the first to clear the crest of the hill, and they froze like a couple of lizards when they got a good look at the valley below. A makeshift guerrilla camp was flourishing in a grove of rubber trees. Yet the more the two men studied the operation the less makeshift did it seem. A huge spreading palapa covered several gun emplacements dug into the hillside. These weapons sites, descending as far as the winding stream on the valley floor, looked highly sophisticated, some of them antiaircraft. What did the rebels think this was, Southeast Asia? Why were they so overarmed? The government wasn't hitting them that hard, was it?

About thirty men moved about the camp, dressed in various combinations of jungle fatigues and jeans and T-shirts—one man had "Bruce is the Boss" printed across his back. Several were armed with AK-47 assault rifles, and a heavy machine-gun emplacement guarded the main approach. It was well protected and hidden from the air by the trees, and clearly larger than most of the highland camps that dotted strategic points throughout the war zone. It was even big by Nicaraguan standards.

And at that moment it was being guarded by just two men.

Schaefer, peering through field binoculars, scanned every inch of the camp below. His observation located one guard standing above the huts on the opposite slope, half asleep in the sun as he squatted over his rifle. Another guard strolled up and down by the machine-gun nest at the main point of entry. It was inexplicable that they didn't have a man stationed on the knoll where Schaefer and Ramirez lay hidden—unless perhaps they had just gotten cocky, having downed a big U.S. chopper the day before. Perhaps they were bloated and a little sleepy, like a snake who's eaten a rat.

In the camp itself Schaefer noticed a guerrilla carrying a hand-held rocket launcher, placing it beside a bandolier of rockets. He also recognized a radio set and consoles that couldn't have come from anywhere else but an American surveillance craft. Schaefer put down his glasses and looked over at Ramirez, who nodded in acknowledgment. He'd picked up the association between the equipment and the downed chopper.

"Seems like we got us some target practice," murmured Schaefer with satisfaction.

"Right on, Major," said Ramirez with a smile. "No women and children neither. We don't have to be too particular, ya know?"

Suddenly their attention was riveted back to the camp at the sound of a muffled cry coming from behind a heavily curtained door on the largest hut. The curtain flew back violently, and a moaning hostage staggered out, shirtless and bleeding from whip wounds all over his upper body. Clearly he'd been beaten severely for hours. His hands were tied behind his back, and he stumbled just outside the door as if kicked from behind. He fell to the ground, feebly trying to maintain his footing. He coughed up a gout of blood and spat it defiantly over his shoulder.

A guerrilla leader emerged from the hut behind him. Tall, mustached, and packing a sidearm, he swaggered over to the beaten hostage, kicking him viciously in the stomach. Then he knelt down beside his victim, withdrew an automatic from his holster, and cocked the hammer slowly as if to prolong the agony. He sneered something in Spanish.

"You go to hell!" choked back the hostage in his captor's tongue. "Go fuck your mother's ass! She's begging for it, man!"

The guerrilla grabbed the man's hair, jammed the nozzle of the gun into his ear, and with a satisfied grin pulled the trigger. The side of the hostage's head exploded all over the curtain in front of the door. Tidiness wasn't in the guerrilla handbook. The leader shoved the dead man's head to the ground and stood up in a kind of macho exultation, gleeful as a bully in a playground. He kicked again at the body as it slumped into a lifeless heap.

Then he slung the pistol back in the holster and turned and walked calmly back into his hut, taking care as he pushed aside the curtain not to soil his fingers in the carnage of blood and brains. The curtain fell back. The corpse lay unattended in the dust. None of the other guerrillas made a move to haul it away. From the look of the camp they weren't really meticulous about any of their garbage.

Schaefer, stonefaced throughout the brutal murder, lowered his glasses, a look of cold determination and hatred on his face.

Ramirez moved to cross himself, and Dutch had to hold himself back from slapping Ramirez's hand aside and pounding his head in the dirt. Ramirez only had a very little bit of religion, a reflex from his childhood and his mother's daily mass, but even a little bit seemed to get under Schaefer's skin.

Quickly the two of them squirmed back down the hillside, joining the others. Schaefer made a circular motion with his forefinger, and the men gathered round him in huddle formation.

Schaefer spoke with calculated rage: "They killed one of the prisoners. I don't know how many they got left. So we take them *now*."

Dillon nodded, as if he was still trying to prove that all orders had to be okayed by him. The rest of the men pointedly ignored him.

Blain and Mac led the way round the hillside, slithering on all fours below the level of the burn, protected by the high grass. As the going got rougher Blain silently slipped out of his cartridge pack and ditched his beloved blaster. Then he withdrew his combat knife and gripped it between his teeth. It was as if he was just as glad to go into this combat hand to hand.

He and Mac rippled through the underbrush in tandem like a pair of stalking tigers—till suddenly Mac froze in mid-creep, the sweat pouring from his streaked face. He held up his hand, signaling Blain to stop. Mac had spotted a hair-thin trip wire. He stretched out an arm and drew a finger along the ground about two inches from the wire till Blain focused on it and nodded.

Mac pointed to where the wire disappeared in a nest of reeds. He bellied over and parted the reeds with his hands, revealing a hidden claymore mine about the size of a pie plate. Grinning in anticipation of twisting the guerrillas' defense mechanism so it would backfire, Mac hunched over the mine and held his breath. Then he redirected the claymore, swiveling it a quarter turn so it faced toward the camp. Then he reattached the wires.

Meanwhile, about a hundred feet downwind, the observer absorbed the cells of a banana palm. It consumed the tree and at the same time replicated it perfectly. In a microsecond there was no tree at all. It was just a thought now in the nerve cluster of the chameleonlike invader, though even the monkeys rutting in the fronds were not aware of the transformation. The blackened bananas looked exactly the same and tasted the same to the flies. The creature sent out its radar, silent as fallout.

It surveyed Blain and Mac with its heat-seeking vision, their bodies outlined in luminous aureoles. To the invader the electrified trip wires with their concentrated energy glowed brilliantly, even under the midday sun, standing out in high-contrast relief to the jungle foliage. The being thought the men must be feeding, drinking up the current like pollinating bees. It could not understand yet what the purpose of these creatures was. Every other species seemed to fit in the scheme of things, and the invader had traveled throughout the universe to study that scheme. It had gathered specimens of each, till they were stacked and filed in its mind like butterflies in a cabinet.

Not man. Man was other, like the alien itself. It was as if the universe had finally dared to think up a proposition equal to the alien's capacity for wonder.

And all it knew was this: it must possess them.

FIVE

As MAC AND BLAIN rewired the mine, Billy had gone ahead at Schaefer's command. Under cover of the bank of the stream he had sneaked his way to within ten feet of the sentry standing guard in the trees beyond the camp. Only the man was on less than red alert, since he was smoking a ganja cigarette and listening to a Walkman through a set of earphones. He swayed slightly to the beat of the music. Like a dart, Billy shot up from the ground, pulling the sentry to him, covering his mouth as he yanked his head backward, dropping him to the ground. With his other hand he plunged his combat knife right under the man's breastbone, killing him instantly. Billy could hear the faint sound of the music leaking out of the earphones. Billy Joel, "Uptown Girl."

"Beware of rock 'n' roll, man," whispered Billy to the dead guerrilla. "It'll turn your brains to mush."

With an unguarded hole now in the southwest corner of the camp, Billy motioned the others forward. Schaefer came up from the bank and passed Billy. When he reached the edge of the trees he went down on his belly again and crawled close to the main entrance, where he took cover behind the rusted skeleton of an

ancient truck. Its rear wheels had been hefted onto concrete blocks, the engine idling slowly. One wheel was
attached to a belt-drive hooked to a pump which was
drawing water from the nearby stream. A second guard
sat in the open cab of the truck, desultorily watching the
high ground above the camp and looking a little woozy
from the gas fumes spewing out of the truck's exhaust.

Another guerrilla beside the truck was attending to
some radio equipment liberated from the U.S. chopper.
He swore a continual stream because the circuits were
too complicated for him. He was a shortwave man, and
his guerrilla training hadn't yet caught up with the com-
puter chip. The man behind the wheel of the truck
slapped at a fly buzzing around his ear and was about to
suggest to the radioman that they break out some Carta
Blanca. They'd done enough for the revolution for one
day.

Just then, hearing a noise from the passenger's side
of the truck, he turned to meet Mac's sledgehammer fist
as it smashed into his throat, severing his windpipe before he could scream. Simultaneously Blain came
around the truck's front fender behind the radioman,
pulling him down and puncturing his chest twice with
his combat knife. The only sound that accompanied either death was a low exhale of breath and a gurgle of
blood in the throat. Mac and Blain prided themselves on
the silence of their technique. Any sort of cry would
have taken all the skill out of it. You couldn't count a
kill that was noisy.

At exactly the same moment Ramirez moved into
position to the side and above the camp. He carefully
checked the readiness of his grenade launcher—six
shots, all loaded. Then he set his MP-5 in front of him,

waiting for a whistle from Schaefer.

Schaefer, meanwhile, had moved to the cab of the truck as Mac and Blain retreated back to the bushes, moving closer to the camp. Schaefer located a satchel charge looped over the gearshift. The truck's engine still rumbled and coughed, and the body of the guerrilla was slumped against the dash in such a way that Schaefer couldn't follow the wiring to its source to destabilize it. If he turned the ignition off someone in the camp would come running. As he peered out from the doorless side of the vehicle, he saw Ramirez signaling to him from the hillside, nearly invisible in the thick brush. Schaefer made a sign like a deaf mute, indicating that Ramirez should take his cue from the truck.

Looking lower down, Schaefer checked to be sure that Dillon and Hawkins were ready. Dillon's binoculars were focused on the machine-gun emplacement. So was Hawkins's rifle. Everybody was in order. Schaefer put two fingers to his lips and gave a short piercing two-note whistle. If the guerrillas had been alert they might have wondered what a blue jay from northern Minnesota was doing in the jungle. But they weren't alert. They were surfeited from the day's triumph, and they were lying belly up and fast asleep, just begging to be attacked.

"Ready, kid?" Dillon asked, turning to Hawkins.

"Yes, sir!" whispered the Irishman excitedly. In a combat situation Hawkins liked a chain of command. He was willing to put aside his former surliness to the black man for the sake of having a superior officer. He did not see it as a contradiction. Before was a power struggle; this was war. Hawkins liked his wars to have rules.

As they slipped through the high grass to the edge of the camp, Schaefer was slicing through the belt-drive with his combat knife. The webbing of the belt was easily half an inch thick, and Dutch was sweating with concentration as he worked the knife. At last it severed the tough fibers, and the end snapped like a whip, and the engine chugged louder. Then Schaefer moved to the rear of the truck and bent down between the wheels like a power lifter about to do a squat.

The truck weighed a ton and a half. Schaefer heaved up, his face beet red with concentration, veins almost bursting his temples as he focused all his strength on deadlifting the truck off its blocks. Pouring every ounce of muscle into the task, his mouth parted in a grimace and a low growl boiled in his throat. Schaefer could feel its rusted springs and frame begin to groan as it shifted off its perch. With a final grunt and thrust he lifted the axle clear of the concrete blocks and heaved it forward. The breath exploded from his mouth in a cry of victory.

The truck lurched forward with a shudder, then slowly lumbered down the hill, its tireless rims digging into the soft earth as Schaefer rolled into cover of the thick vegetation by the river.

As the truck gathered speed and sound, one of the guerrillas looked up the hill with sudden alarm, startled to see the rattling vehicle bearing down on the camp. Barking orders to several comrades he gathered a small group of surprised men who scurried up the slope to try to stop it. But it rolled faster and faster toward the clearing, uprooting plants and spitting stones as it barreled headlong. It was heading toward the main palapa.

The guerrillas' outstretched arms, holding hands like students at a rally, made a fruitless attempt to slow the truck's progress. It flung them aside like toy soldiers and smashed through the front wall, collapsing the thatch roof and bursting through the other side, shattered stalks of bamboo walls and war-room furniture exploding in its path across the clearing.

A half dozen bewildered guerrillas turned and looked back up the hill, searching for something to explain the freak disaster. As they stood there stunned Schaefer was a beat ahead of them. He pulled the pin of a pinecone grenade and footballed it into the air. It arced dead center for the camp, spiraling above the guerrillas' heads, then bounced on the ground twice before it rolled into the fuel dump. There was a moment's agonizing pause, during which even the jungle twitterers seemed to hold their breath. Then the grenade blew, igniting the fuel, and the dump exploded in an incredible fireball, roaring yellow and orange with thunderous crashes. Shrapnel whizzed in all directions, razoring a guerrilla's arm at the elbow, blinding another in one eye.

The banana palm on the downhill slope suddenly seemed to shrivel. The alien withdrew to the safety of the ground as if it couldn't bear the intensity of what was starting to happen. Its optic cells were blinded by the white-hot flashes of the explosion, its heat-sensitive radar temporarily overwhelmed. Power like this made it frightened of men, and it hated to be frightened. It had its own code, if nothing so real as pride or honor. It simply could not tolerate any power more explosive than its own, so it sank into itself to figure out a strategy. It had to win, even here on this weakling planet whose creatures were bent on destroying one another.

As a score of confused men scattered out of the various huts a second explosion sounded, this one caused by the satchel in the truck as it detonated with an ear-splitting roar. The truck smithereened into fragments of steel which shot through the camp like a shrapnel bomb. Two huts collapsed into puffs of straw. Three men were torn up as they ran, and only two of them died right away.

As soon as the explosion settled, Schaefer came darting down the slope in the truck's path, taking advantage of the dazed state of the rebels. Without aiming at anyone in particular, he tore off round after round with his M-203, wounding and killing several guerrillas as they staggered about.

As Hawkins and Dillon ran down, leaving Ramirez behind to cover them, some of the guerrillas had recovered their wits and jumped to man their weapons. Bullets burst at Hawkins's and Dillon's feet as they closed in on Schaefer to form a wedge. Schaefer slammed another round of 40mm cartridges into his gun, and the three men sprayed fire.

Blain and Mac erupted out of the bushes behind the main hut, a withering curtain of lead on the right flank. So now the commandos were coming in like a pincers from both sides, and the guerrillas didn't know where to aim. Mac gutted a hulking fullback with his combat knife, then spun around and slit another man's throat with his backswing.

They were basically ripping the camp to shreds. A guerrilla lieutenant, futilely trying to bark orders, let out a blood-curdling scream as his clothes and skin went up in flames from a direct grenade hit. He dived into the jungle and flailed about, blazing in phosphorous flames.

Ramirez, poised on the slope with his grenade launcher, kept lobbing his missiles behind the camp so none of the enemy could slip through and escape across the stream. Suddenly he sighted two guerrillas diving into position at the machine gun emplacement. Frantically they worked to load the chamber, but just as they swung to aim at the left flank of the commando assault, Ramirez let loose with a double grenade. At the exact moment that the guerrilla got Schaefer, Dillon, and Hawkins in his sights, his head blew off. As the grenades detonated and took the machine-gun ammo with them the whole bunker blew twenty feet into the air, making hamburger out of the two guerrillas.

In one of the few remaining huts, a terrified rebel took shaky aim at Schaefer as the major stopped to reload. Just in time Dillon noticed him about to open fire, and he screamed a warning to Dutch.

"Right shoulder!"

Instantly Schaefer hit the ground as a shroud of bullets passed inches above his head. But even as he flattened against the turf he rolled and fired the 203, completely destroying the hut and the enemy gunners as well.

High on the hill above the smoking battleground a jackal peered out of a shallow cave, cautious and alert. Or at least it was a jackal a minute ago. Now, if you came up close and looked in its yellow eyes, you would have observed the faintest network of scales, as if the eye was composed of thousands of minute chambers intricate as a beehive.

For the alien had advanced again. Now for the first time it occupied the body of a hot-blooded mammal. From a single patch of jackal hair snagged by a branch at the mouth of the cave the alien had replicated with a massive surge of power, and now its matted coat twitched away the jungle flies as it watched the carnage below. It liked the feel of blood in its veins. It even felt a kind of kinship to the mad warrior running riot in the camp.

Its eyes slowly adjusted to the explosive blasts that had earlier seemed to blind it. An eerie, surreal kaleidoscope unfolded as its heat vision scanned the camp. Screams of mutilation and pain echoed through the jungle as laserlike rockets zapped in all directions, reducing men and equipment to ruin.

One of the last surviving guerrillas stood in the entrance to the main palapa, covering his comrades as they fell back inside. It was the captain who'd performed the execution. Billy, who'd been scrabbling across the roof of the hut immediately adjacent, jumped down and landed directly in front of the armed man, who swung his gun around towards the Indian.

Just then, another guerrilla rushed around the corner of the hut, slashing out at Billy with his combat knife, razoring his cheek. Spinning like a scorpion Billy whipped his arm around the guerrilla's chest, locking his elbow in a cracking motion and using the man as a shield when the captain fired, thus spilling his own comrade's guts. Then Billy pointed the tip of his shotgun at the startled captain's face and blew him off his feet. He released his hold on the dead man, and the body collapsed just where the executed man had fallen earlier. But you could no longer tell whose blood was whose.

Billy stepped over the dead rebels, threw back the curtain and raced down the stairs, firing indiscriminately. He had no fear for himself. He was determined to eliminate anyone left in the main stronghold, and he seemed to move in a kind of magic circle of protection. No one was going to stop him.

Meanwhile, Blain crept forward to the entrance, providing cover for Billy while the Indian cleaned out the hut. Blain didn't notice the crouching guerrilla circling behind him at the edge of the stream. The guerrilla fired a grenade round which exploded at Blain's feet, fragments of shrapnel ripping into his vest.

One jagged flash of metal lodged in his shoulder. But as the present danger didn't allow the luxury of responding to excruciating pain, Blain just narrowed his eyes and dutifully swiveled around, growling savagely as he opened fire in a back and forth motion, ripping through the enemy soldier till he was a bloody lump of dying flesh bleeding into the water.

Then Mac charged out of the jungle as if some instinct had told him his buddy was wounded. Blain flashed him a peace sign and grinned, completely shrugging off the blood that seeped down the arm of his khaki shirt. *Hey, what's a little blood?* he seemed to be saying.

The jungle clearing was suddenly deathly quiet. Apparently they were all either blown away or had fled into the trees. The commandos began to close in on the main palapa. They could hear the sporadic firing of Billy's rifle in the underground bunker as he nosed around, but there didn't seem to be any guerrillas left. They regrouped by the door, glancing quickly at one another to make sure they were still in one piece. Ramirez had bloodied his lip hitting the dirt, but otherwise Blain's was the only injury.

"Looks like a fuckin' Purple Heart to me," cracked Mac as he eyed Blain's shoulder.

"Yo, Billy!" called Schaefer into the palapa. "What you got down there?"

"Looks like the friggin' Pentagon, Major," Billy shouted back—but just as he finished speaking there was a burst of machine-gun fire in the bunker.

Schaefer and Ramirez bolted in and ran down the crude stairs. The palapa was dug deeply into the soft earth, the walls reinforced with sandbags. A string of electric bulbs zigzagged across the trench at about shoulder height, powered by a small generator that wheezed and sighed in one corner. The underground space was maybe thirty by fifty feet, partitioned off by stacks of wooden crates full of supplies. It looked like the cellar of a hardware store.

Schaefer and Ramirez darted between the aisles, sweeping every shadowy corner with their rifles cocked. About twenty feet along the center aisle was a door in the wall of earth. Savagely Schaefer kicked it open. He suddenly faced a wide-eyed guerrilla whom he flattened with a single bullet to the brain, since he wasn't in the mood to talk.

He and Ramirez hopped over the dead man and surveyed a long corridor that tunneled deep into the earth toward the stream. At the far end was another stairway which obviously led to an escape route. The two commandos barreled down the corridor just in time to see a wild-eyed rebel struggling to open the hatch. Ramirez tore off a full burst of bullets that exploded into the fleeing man. The force spun him around, and he took a last opportunity to fire, sending a scattering of bullets into the earthen roof which rained down dirt on the commandos' heads. Then the rebel fell dead at the foot of the steps.

Schaefer and Ramirez turned and headed back to the main chamber. As they came around into the central aisle a wounded man was crawling behind a stack of crates, dragging a bloody leg. Schaefer and Ramirez ducked as he drew down on them with a machine pistol. Schaefer heaved at the pile of crates and tipped it over, crashing several hundred pounds of ordinance on top of the man. The machine bullets veered off target.

Then Schaefer rushed on the guy and bashed his head with the butt of his rifle, knocking him senseless.

Jamming in a new clip the major scanned the palapa for other movements, then nodded to Ramirez to proceed along the aisle. Catlike, Ramirez covered the last twenty feet and came on a couple of bodies heaped at the foot of a last set of stairs that disappeared up into the jungle. There was no telling how many had escaped this way, though Billy had clearly nailed the two who hadn't.

"Billy musta gone up after 'em," Ramirez called back to the major. "I'll go cover his ass."

And he raced up the steps and disappeared into the trees. Dutch wasn't worried about either of them. He'd rather have his men out there hounding the enemy to earth than wait and let the guerrillas creep back for a second round. Up above in the clearing Schaefer could hear Hawkins barking into the radio as Mac and Blain set up the portable satellite dish antenna.

Otherwise there was stillness.

SIX

AFTER THE SUDDEN gunfire and commotion the camp had taken on the aura of postwar calm, tense as the eye of a hurricane. The blasts and explosions had frightened all wildlife away or into silence, and the pulse of the jungle was weirdly flat in the oppressive heat of the late afternoon.

Gazing around the palapa, Schaefer silently observed heaps of helmets and battle gear and crateloads of ammunition by the score. For the first time he was able to study the methodically warehoused interior of the cavernous chamber, the enormous stockpiles of weapons and equipment. It was obviously a major military stronghold, doubly so to be so deep in the mountains. It had taken weeks and a lot of money to cart all this shit in. They had enough combat supplies in here to level Brazil.

As he finished a cursory inventory and headed up the steps to the clearing he wondered why they had centralized such a reservoir of sophisticated equipment. He figured most of it was stolen from ship's cargos en route to opposing armies, or bartered from shaky third world regimes that supported the attempted takeover. But already he realized there had to be a reason, a highly explosive reason, to go to all this trouble to arm a camp in the middle of nowhere. Even as he absorbed the evidence, his instincts began to shiver with suspicions he couldn't yet identify or explain. But as he threw back the curtain and stepped out into the clearing Dillon came to mind with a sour taste. He filed another red flag as Mac jogged over to him.

"Any sign of the hostages?" Schaefer inquired with narrowed eyes.

Mac was agitated. "We found all three of 'em, Major. Dead." He pointed across the clearing to one of the huts. "The gear from the chopper too. Listen, if those guys are Central American, I'm a fuckin' Chinaman. By the look of 'em I'd say CIA."

Schaefer's eyes were like slits as he darted a look at Dillon, who huddled over the radio next to Hawkins, trying to shout their coordinates.

"Oh, another thing, Major," Mac added. "We got lucky. Couple these guys we waxed are Russians. Got their transport papers right in their hip pocket. Some kinda counterespionage unit. There was major shit about to get goin' here."

As Schaefer listened to Mac's casual speculations his face began to tighten and redden with anger. The fragmented image of his vague suspicions began to take a shape. But still he kept his thoughts to himself, not revealing a glimmer of a reaction to Mac's brute irony.

"Good work, Mac," he said brusquely. "Clear the area—no traces. Then get the men ready to move."

Blain had been nosing among the flattened huts, and now he whistled to the major, hailing Schaefer with the wave of an arm. *Now what,* Schaefer thought grimly as he stepped around Dillon and Hawkins hunched at the radio and crossed through the blasted wreckage of the huts. Blain was pointing his cocked rifle at the inert form of a guerrilla who lay in the twisted thatchwork. The enemy wore fatigues and a cap that hid most of his face, but even the hard army clothes didn't hide the fact that this contra was hardly out of his mid-teens. It crossed Schaefer's mind as it had in Indochina: kids did the dying in hopeless wars.

"He's still breathin'," Blain said flatly, as unsentimental about enemy kids as he was about everything else. Blain's world was good guys and bad guys. There were no good bad guys.

Schaefer waved him away, then pulled out his revolver. Carefully he rolled out the chamber and with the swift technique of a combat vet he filled it with six lead bullets. Then he knelt beside the enemy soldier. This kid, he was thinking, might have some answers his captains didn't even know—if he could be revived. Schaefer lifted the boy's hand to check for pulse. It was, oddly, a narrow hand with long tapered fingers, delicate yet strong. The major's eyes moved up to the face, now visible under the cap—the face of a girl.

Probably in her mid-twenties, her hair tied back and tucked under the cap, she looked lost in the loose-fitting fatigues. Because of the clothes, and with her cheeks streaked with dirt and blood, it was no wonder Blain hadn't noticed her gender.

Schaefer stared at her intently, as if he couldn't make this fit with the three bodies flayed and hanging from the tree, even though he had seen children toss bombs and run away laughing. She was beautiful with a tawny complexion and thick black hair. She had a strong narrow face, the jaw tight and the sensuous mouth pouting defiantly. Even as she lay unconscious he could see the rebellious spirit in her expression. The haughty romantic, the angry commitment to the cause would be there when she awoke, he knew.

Schaefer was well aware that for a woman to be on active duty in the top rebel force in this chauvinistic, Catholic backwater of a country—where the men really did keep their women barefoot and pregnant—this had to be one extraordinarily talented and well-connected lady. As much as he despised the barbaric tactics and the inhuman style of the rebels, he had to smile a little here, as if with a momentary glint of respect.

Her pulse was stable. He pulled off the cap and turned her head. Apparently she had been knocked unconscious by the falling roof of the hut, but there was no evidence of serious injury other than a nasty head gash. She'd be all right.

As an automatic precaution he picked up the pistol she'd dropped at her side and ejected the clip. Then, with a hunger for some answers, he began to rummage through papers scattered in the wreckage around her, impatient for information about the place he had just destroyed. Frustrated and tired, he tossed the irrelevant sheets of paper back on the ground—lists of supplies in Spanish, newspapers, propaganda leaflets. Then suddenly he paused at one torn page in his hand and began reading intently.

It was a form he couldn't translate entirely, but one he knew the meaning of immediately. It was orders to launch a major offensive on the Conta Mana capital; to level the city if need be—no prisoners, mass execution. Schaefer had seen the same kind of combat orders in five different languages. People always blew their country up in words that fit on a single page. And according to the document the whole offensive was to begin in just three days.

The pieces began to fall together. Suddenly Schaefer realized he was standing at the epicenter of the guerrillas' pivotal invasion tactic. The war that had been just skirmishes and incidents—pipe bombs thrown in alleys, peasants disappeared—was about to become a full-scale conflagration on the international scale. The tough-guy munitions and radar equipment littered the jungle camp like the remnants of a lost culture that prayed to a deaf god. Before Schaefer and his men had barreled in it was all poised to stream through the jungle toward a final battle.

It was clear as day now: Phillips's so-called mission to rescue three politicos was a ruse to manipulate Schaefer and his men to block the rebel invasion. Dillon, Phillips, the full fucking central command—they all must've gotten wind of the plan before Schaefer was ever summoned.

Oh, yes. Schaefer was going to get some answers now. And then he would cram them down everyone's throat all the way from here to Langley.

Ramirez moved lightly among the rubber trees, chasing a bunch of rebels who'd managed to escape. They were so sloppy in their scramble to retreat that they left a trail a Girl Scout could have followed. The moss was torn and the lower branches trampled. One of the guerrillas had dropped a revolver by the stump of a tree, as if even weapons were a burden now. These last survivors of the camp just wanted out.

Maneuvering through a thicket, Ramirez emerged into a small clearing. At the far edge was a sheer cliff shooting up about fifty feet, with a trickle of water trailing scum across the face of the rock. At the top was a ledge which trailed off to another level of jungle. As Ramirez approached the dead-end spot at the base of the cliff he could see that the rock was hollowed out here and there with shallow caves, the trails of moss and slime half obscuring the openings.

Suddenly he noticed movement above, and he ducked behind an outcropping of rock just as the echoing zing of bullets careened off the ground around him. One of the bullets grazed his upper arm as he leaped for the protection of a larger boulder. From there he could see that at least two guerrillas had taken cover in the cliff hollows.

As one of them crouched to reload, thinking Ramirez was down, the commando took aim and returned the fire. He clipped the guerrilla on the side of the head before he could duck in the cave. The rebel screamed once, then toppled backward down the rock face, hitting the mossy ground below about five feet from Ramirez. The Chicano hastily crossed himself, thinking as he stared in the dead man's eyes how they could've been cousins. Ramirez didn't like killing brown men, not unless they lived in the Middle East.

The other rebel was still holed up in a higher cave with better protection. With the advantage of elevation over Ramirez he was able to keep the commando pinned behind the boulder with minimum fire. The feisty Chicano quickly shook his brotherly feelings. He hated being treated like a cornered rat.

Just then Blain broke through the underbrush, hesitating before he entered the clearing. Ramirez, making eye contact, motioned to the dead man, then up above to the enemy, alerting his buddy so he wouldn't stumble into a downpour of bullets. Then he made a beckoning motion, indicating he would cover Blain so the latter could join him behind the boulder. Knowing the rebel would hunker down in the cave under rapid fire, Ramirez opened up, making the trails of moss dance along the cliff face and giving Blain the precious seconds to run to his side.

Right away, Ramirez noticed Blain's torn and bloody shirt. "You shithead, you're hit! You're bleedin' all over me, man!"

"Goddam grenade blew while I was coverin' Billy," the big man explained, glancing down at the caking blood. "Anyway, I ain't got time to bleed."

He was right about the time. Half a second later a grenade exploded a few feet away, blowing a leg off the dead rebel. A round of automatic fire followed. The spray of dirt coughed up was as thick as a Saigon mud storm.

As the grit settled on the two commandos Ramirez quickly replaced the 40mm rounds in his six-shooter. Then he leaped over the boulder and threw himself into the line of fire.

"Come back here, you stupid spic!" shouted Blain.

Ramirez blasted six rapid-fire rounds on a high-arc trajectory toward the enemy cave above. Then, just as quick as he went, he scrambled back to the protection of the rock, squatting next to Blain.

"We call that a Tijuana yoyo," he said, then grinned as he popped his fingers in his ears.

Blain grimaced and ducked his head—just as the whole cliffside exploded.

An instant later enormous chunks of rock rumbled

down like meteorites. Then a torrent of vegetation rained down on their heads, mixed with the dying screams of several rebels holed up in the cliff. For a few long seconds nothing was visible but the avalanche of shredded jungle matter pouring into the vortex. The stream on the rock face spewed like a broken hose. Then a dead calm followed like a windless sea, and the jungle froze. For half a mile around nothing made a peep.

Then Blain's voice rose from the wreckage. "You stupid spic!" he crowed, but this time it was a cry of triumph.

Schaefer still stood by the unconscious woman, his weapon hanging slack from one arm, the telling paper clenched in his fingers as if it were the pivotal evidence in a sensational trial. Except here in the jungle waste there was neither judge nor jury, and the only law that worked lay crouched in the bush, ready to spring for the throat.

Dutch stared silently fuming at the ruined huts. He didn't notice the black man moving toward him, poking at the ground for classified stuff. Dillon scarcely looked at the girl as he knelt and began sorting through the papers Schaefer had already scoured. Dutch made no attempt to tell him he was wasting his time. He simply watched the back of the black man's head for a long moment, trying to remember exactly where it was in Indochina that he'd felt the blood bond for his comrade. Sometimes the countries just seemed to blur—dirty and thick with flies, the sick whores and the rotten politicians, the wars that went on for decades.

Dillon broke the silence. "We did it, Dutch, we did

it," he said excitedly, methodically sorting through stacks of paper. He might have been sitting at his desk at that moment. Every scrap of paper seemed to have meaning to him—even the bills for printing the antigovernment posters. "This is beautiful!" he exclaimed. "More than we even expected. We got the bastards cold!"

Schaefer crouched, leaned across the body of the unconscious girl, and handed Dillon the one sheet he had culled from the mess. "Hey pal, I think *this* is the one you're lookin' for," said the major with a steely edge.

Dillon took the paper and read intently, his eyes widening. "Three days—that's all we had," he said with a shake of his head. "Not a fuckin' minute to waste, Dutch. In three days you would've had hundreds of these geeks in here. Equipped up the ass," he added, sweeping his hand and taking in the entire routed camp. "Once they crossed the border they would've been home free. It'd take a year to stop 'em."

Dillon put a solemn hand on Schaefer's shoulder and continued sanctimoniously. "You guys have averted a major rebel invasion, Dutch. They're gonna know about this all the way to the Big House, I promise you."

Schaefer stood abruptly, throwing off Dillon's hand. His eyes narrowed, his nostrils flared, and he stared defiantly into the black man's face. Venom seethed through his words. "It was all bullshit—*all* of it! Right from the start, huh? *You* set us up," he sneered. "Brought us in here to fight your dirty little nonpartisan war. I guess we're what you call technical advisers— ain't that the polite word for it, or have you figured out somethin' even better? Somethin' that makes your shit smell real clean, right? You fuckin' sonuvabitch!"

Dillon retorted angrily. "Hey gimme a break, Dutch. So the Company set you up. So who do you believe in—the Easter Bunny? We had a goddam good reason. You're the best there is, Dutch. I needed you."

"Why the fuck didn't you tell me what was goin' down?"

Dillon shrugged. It was the shrug of every bureaucrat the world over. "Couldn't, Dutch. Had little blue tags all over it—National Security, White House only. I didn't even know all the details myself till I was on the plane. They asked me who could take out a guerrilla camp, and I said you guys. I had to give you a cover story. Orders right from the Oval Office—swear to God, Dutch."

"Remind me to pledge allegiance next time we pass a flag."

"You got a right to be pissed. I'm not sayin' you don't."

"That's real sportin' of you, pal. And one other thing—what kinda story did you tell Jack Davis?"

Dillon winced, recalling the three horribly mutilated men they'd found earlier. "Dutch, you've got to understand, we been trying to find this place for months. Davis was sent in to pull the CIA guys once they had a fix on the camp. He volunteered for the job. But he must've gotten careless. Flew too close, and they shot him down. When he disappeared I had to clean up and stop these bastards. We were so close we couldn't quit." Dillon's tone had softened. It was more like plea bargaining than righteous indignation. "We couldn't sleep through this one, Dutch. You were the only guy I could trust."

"To invade a foreign country. Illegally." Schaefer

spoke cold as a prosecutor, savoring the affront to international law. "You lied, pal—that's all it comes down to. You stacked the odds and set us up. You could've gotten every one of us killed. We could be rottin' our asses off in tiger cages for the duration of the fuckin' conflict, and nobody would even know except the White House. Gee, you think maybe him and Nancy'd remember us in their prayers—like when they're sayin' grace at dinner, and maybe there's a picture of Lincoln on the wall?"

He paused a moment, breathing heavy from the rage and feeling a dryness in his throat like he'd give his right thumb for a Carta Blanca. With huge contempt he spat out the next words.

"You used to be one of us, Dillon. I think maybe we were drinkin' buddies too, but I must've been really in the bag, 'cause I mixed you up with this guy who saved my ass once. I don't know who the fuck *you* are."

No one was going to win this tennis match. The ball had been smashed to smithereens.

"We've been through a lot together, Dutch," Dillon replied quietly, still groping for a way to unplug Schaefer's rage. "We were the best. But hey, things changed. We're fighting these Marxist wackos in a dozen fuckin' countries, and they're gettin' closer. This isn't the rice paddies anymore. We're three hours from Texas. We lose *this* fight, Dutch, and they start playin' the game with buttons. We're all expendable assets, Major. Can't you see that?"

Schaefer snapped the document out of Dillon's hand. "That's your problem, Dillon," he said. "And I'll tell you somethin' else—your last stand for democracy and a quarter wouldn't buy me a fuckin' Hershey bar. What it's always about for you is gettin' ahead, isn't it? You gotta be the first black president or else. Who cares about a bunch of off-the-wall commandos? They gotta die sometime, right? Well, listen good, dude—my men are not expendable. We don't do this kind of work."

Schaefer crumpled the paper in his fist. "This is *your* dirty little war, not mine!" Then he stuffed the wad into Dillon's shirt pocket and walked away.

Dillon didn't move for a moment. He let the wad of paper sit in his breast pocket. He knew where he stood with Schaefer now, but in any case there was no more time to waste. He bent to sift again through the papers.

SEVEN

SCHAEFER CAME UP behind Hawkins and watched him tap at the radio dials. He was angry more for his men than for himself. Schaefer was a loyalist, the kind of leader who would defend his last man if it meant his own life, no matter what. There were disadvantages to such loyalty, of course, and getting hooked into deals like this was where it sometimes got you. Schaefer knew he couldn't just walk, not with five men depending on him, and not in the middle of nowhere. He had to get all of them out somehow. For he didn't trust anybody else to do it for him now—not the company, not the White House, especially not Dillon.

As for the problem of Dillon, the major knew that, though he himself had a keen sense of other men's limits and loyalties, he had one glaring flaw: he believed that combat experience made everyone as tough as he was, and he expected as much integrity as he delivered. And that kind of standards sometimes led to bitter disappointment, or worse. Dillon had treaded on a territory that bordered on the double-cross, offending Schaefer irreversibly. Rank was academic at this point. If Dillon had tried to give him an order just then, he would have responded with a contemptuous laugh.

While Dillon went on rifling through the papers, the woman on the ground beside him groaned as she began to regain consciousness. A thin trickle of blood from the head wound matted her hair and ran down the side of her cheek. She began mumbling incoherently in Spanish. It sounded like a prayer. Dillon knelt down next to her and began rummaging through her pockets. He retrieved a thin nylon billfold and pulled out an identification card. Beneath a list of serial numbers was her name: "Anna Gonsalves." No rank noted.

Hawkins had set up the field radio on a crate just outside the palapa door. Though he had reattached the wires three times he was getting very garbled reception. He listened carefully, every few moments tapping his talk button and saying loudly: "Again. Say it again." Finally he looked up at Schaefer.

"Major, we just stepped in some real shit here. I got a hookup with aerial surv." His voice was strained, and the sweat was pouring down his face from concentration.

"Any movement?" asked Schaefer impatiently.

"Everywhere. The whole fuckin' country seems to be bustin' ass to get here. Rebels must've got word out they were bein' attacked."

"How much time?" Schaefer pressed.

"Half an hour, tops. Then this place is gonna be crawling with them apes."

The major tapped Hawkins lightly on the shoulder in a gesture that managed to be equal parts reassurance and appreciation. "Good work, Hawk. Go find Mac and tell him we move in five."

Schaefer knew he had to deal again with Dillon, and

as he walked across the wreckage toward the black man he could see that the girl was sitting up. She held the side of her head in one cupped hand. Her eyes were open, but she was clearly still in a daze. Dillon was bending over her asking a question she didn't seem to hear.

The black man looked up as Schaefer reached them. The major's eyes were glazed with suspicion and disdain, but Dillon seemed to have put the disagreement behind him. "She goes with us," he stated flatly.

"Hey, she doesn't need us to save her." Schaefer's voice was dry. "She's gonna have about a thousand friends here in half an hour."

"Sorry, Dutch, she's too valuable. She's gotta know their whole network." Dillon couldn't keep the excitement out of his voice. "What she knows could mean the lives of thousands of people. We take her with us," he repeated precisely. This time it sounded like an order.

Schaefer held out a massive fist, thumb pointing to the ground. His lower lip curled with suppressed fury. "We take her and she'll give away our position," he countered tightly. "Every chance she gets. No prisoners."

They were sparring with something here that was bigger than logistics. There was a deep rift between them now with the details of the mission revealed. They both knew how far down two opposite roads they'd traveled since they last saw each other. The sparks flying between them couldn't hide what seemed like an underlying sense of pity they felt for each other. Dillon simply couldn't understand why Schaefer still held to an old code that a new kind of war had left far behind. For his part Schaefer was feeling as if he had enemy troops coming at him from both sides—or was it two different kinds of enemy, one inside and one outside, and Dillon was some kind of go-between?

Dillon walked past Schaefer and strode to the radio hookup and grabbed the handset. He held it out to Schaefer and spoke across the ruins. "You're still under orders, Dutch," he said coldly, pulling rank at last. "You want to make the call or should I?"

Schaefer stared at him, then down at the dazed girl. He knew Dillon had this round won. There was nothing Dutch could do about it while he still had responsibility for the commando team. But he wouldn't give Dillon the satisfaction of a verbal response. He simply turned and walked away.

"I'm getting my men outa this fuckin' pit, Dillon," he growled. "*That's* the mission now. The broad's your baggage. You fall behind, you're on your own!"

It was a precarious and potentially dangerous stand-off. Dillon was in nominal charge of the evacuation, but he knew his life depended on the major's cooperation. At this point Dillon's seniority counted for little more than the couple of extra stripes on his shoulder, and the shoulder was liable to get very bloody at any moment. So he simply let the challenge slide and assumed all further responsibility for the prisoner.

Perhaps it seemed like a fair enough trade to the black man since he was going to get all the glory once she had been debriefed. Meanwhile, he could handle Schaefer's anger. He had no doubt the major would bring them safely out of here, and after that he and Schaefer would be off again on those opposite roads. To each his own.

Still, the mission had radically changed focus for all

of them. Now they had one overriding goal: get every-one out of the jungle, safe and soon.

Schaefer knelt in the kicked-up turf by the trailhead, studying a map of the border terrain that Blain had re-trieved from the palapa. Billy, who crouched beside him, had reconnoitered about a mile upstream, and now he pointed to several features on the coded map and fleshed out details of the terrain to the north and west. The rest of the commandos were ranged behind them, covering all entrances to the camp—eyes darting, weapons cocked.

"This place is too hot for a pickup," Schaefer grum-bled. "That's what you're saying, isn't it?"

Billy nodded. The major had already talked to a cou-ple of U.S. choppers standing by just over the border. They'd radioed to Hawkins that they were less than ten miles away—miles that under these conditions might as well have been in Siberia.

"They won't touch us till we're over the border," declared Schaefer. "They made that real clear. They don't want to be tracked in Conta Mana airspace. Fas-tidious buggers, aren't they?"

"Major, look," said Billy, "we can lift at LZ 49, right here." The Indian pointed to a pale green clearing on the contour map just over the border. "But it'll be awful tough going," he added grimly, moving his finger along a stretch of heavily shaded concentric circles that indi-cated steep terrain. "It's all box canyons except for this valley." And he traced lightly along a narrow passage above the head of the stream where the shading of the map was slightly paler.

Dutch whistled Ramirez over and sketched out the

route. Though he trusted Billy's instincts over any map
he needed to get the navigator's view, for Ramirez
would set the pace while Billy scouted ahead, and they
weren't going to get anywhere if the two men weren't in
synch. Billy and Ramirez had to gauge each other by an
inner radar or else they were lost.

Shaking his head, Ramirez spat out the butt of his
cigar. "Well, it ain't the prettiest trip I ever took, Major.
In fact it's gonna be a real bitch." He eyed the jungle
valley as Schaefer's finger traced it. "But if we can get
above the river and then go down this gradient here—
yeah, we might find our way out." He rapped the spot
with his forefinger, then looked over at Billy with a
crooked grin and said: "I suppose this is your idea,
Tonto."

Schaefer, absorbing Billy's and Ramirez's agreement, gritted his teeth and inhaled deeply. "Not much
choice, Pancho, right? Take the lead. Double time it,"
he ordered, anxious now, as if they'd wasted too much
time on maps. He waved an arm, signaling the men to
join ranks.

As the commandos hustled to the trailhead Dillon
came walking up with Anna, her head wrapped in a
strip of cloth torn from a dead guerrilla's shirt. Dillon
had secured her hands in front. As Schaefer watched
them approach he was struck more forcefully than ever
by her raw, reckless beauty now that she was walking
upright for the first time. She was tall and svelte, with a
taut sleek body like a panther—more like an Amazon
warrior than the squat, thick women of her country.

For ventilation in the sweltering heat, she'd unbut-
toned the lower snaps on her fatigue shirt and tied the
ends together, exposing her flat brown stomach and em-

phasizing her breasts. Her eyes were bright and alert, and her upper lip quivered with contempt and hatred at the men who had captured her and killed her comrades.

Schaefer took it all in, registered trouble, then turned back to the others as he organized their retreat. "Lock 'n' load," he instructed gruffly. "Watch your ass."

Immediately Blain moved out, swinging the machine gun in front of him to throw his weight forward up the hill. Then Hawkins with the radio on his back. Everybody wanted out, sensing the impending arrival of the rebel forces, knowing from their own rage how insanely angry the guerrillas would be.

Dillon gently prodded the woman forward onto the trail. The moment he touched her she spun around, hurling a stream of insults at him in Spanish.

"Yankee scum!" she snarled. "You touch me again, you pig, and I'll cut off your balls!"

Dillon was in for it, all right, but he was determined to take it in stride. "It's a long walk back, honey," he replied evenly. "Make it easy on yourself."

She hissed like a cat and spat at his feet, then turned to the trail with a violent twist of her head. Her long black hair, twined in a thick braid which had come loose from under her cap, slapped him across the face.

Dillon silently counted ten, bent over, and slipped his pack over his shoulder and headed out, ignoring her further outbursts. As they followed the others a voice called out in a loud whisper from behind and to the right.

"Hey, Dillon! Over here!"

Dillon knew it was Mac and didn't respond. He didn't want to hear another insubordinate jibe about the prisoner. So Mac called louder.

"Dillon, I said *over here!*"

This time the black man turned coldly to acknowledge his hulking comrade, still holding the girl by the rope that bound her wrists. Mac crouched at the edge of the underbrush with glittering eyes, a wild astonished grin on his face. He was staring at Dillon's shoulder, as if he was going to tease the black man about his rank stripes. "Yeah, what is it, Sergeant?" Dillon asked, visibly annoyed.

Without a word Mac unsheathed his knife, gave Dillon an antic look, and turned him around by his shoulders with an air of condescension. Crawling across the strap of Dillon's pack was a four-inch scorpion, its tail quivering. With a self-satisfied smile, Mac skewered the lethal insect on the tip of his blade and displayed its writhing death throes in front of Dillon's wincing face. Anna smirked, nodding at the disemboweled creature.

"When my people catch you, you'll wish you were *him!*" she declared with a triumphant smile that was the match of Mac's own.

Dillon murmured his thanks to Mac, embarrassed and vaguely insulted, while still trying to ignore Anna's badgering.

"Any time, sir," Mac responded with casual disinterest. Then, as if to wring every ounce of irony from the incident, he flung the scorpion to the ground and crunched it with his boot. He turned and strode ahead, as if to leave the women and the noncombatants to bring up the rear. Dillon followed with a weary sigh, tugging Anna along behind him.

As the small troop moved forward, Billy pulled up at the tail, furtively glancing behind him every few sec-

onds. Since the first mile or so was clearly marked,
having been used to haul equipment, Hawkins wouldn't
need him to scout ahead till they came to the first
rapids. Billy often covered the team's retreat, so there
wasn't anything unusual about his dropping back with
his ears perked. But he seemed strangely agitated, and
he was breathing faster than a man in his shape ought
to.

He sensed a peculiar presence more strongly now
than when he was in the crevasse, and it made his skin
crawl. Something inexplicably familiar yet unknown.
Slowly he scanned the treeline, straining his eyes to
catch a hint of something different, something off-key.
A force was out there among the trees, waiting, watching, Billy was convinced of it; never had his nerves
been so rattled, his brain so wired. Then, oddly, the
jungle began to grow silent. The incessant chirping and
clattering of millions of insects and birds—Billy could
almost feel the volume turning down, as if it was something in his own head that was warning the world to
watch out.

Billy turned and trotted away up the trail, heavy with
dread. He seemed to want to put as much distance as
possible now between him and the carnage of the rebel
camp. Another soldier might have called it just another
case of the spooks. Commando or not, a good fighter
left death behind as quick as he could, or else maybe he
wouldn't get up to fight tomorrow.

But it wasn't the bodies bloating in the heat in the
ruined camp. It wasn't the circling vultures, or the rats
and worms and flies gathering to feed. It was worse
than all the minions of death.

Far up in the tallest cottonwood, high above the

wreckage of the camp, the alien had taken in every in-
finitesimal movement the team had made. As the men
exited the site and disappeared into the trees it uttered a
low trill as it sprang from the tent of leaves into the
humid air, sweeping across to a lower branch in a neigh-
boring tree.

In that horrible moment it was clear at last that the
invader had found a form. Etched against the tropical
sky it was humanoid and vast, seven feet tall with ice-
blue scales from head to foot, and it swung from tree to
tree with the brachiating ease of a golden gorilla. It
wasn't man exactly but a vision of a man, tortured and
perfected by a mind that longed to advance the species
and make it triumph in the jungle habitat. Replication
wasn't good enough. In homage to the warriors it had
tracked all day it sought a shape deep in itself. As if to
fight them to the death it had to be itself and them all at
once.

Skillfully and silently, with fluidlike grace, the creature descended branch to branch till it reached the jungle
floor. As its powerful three-toed feet flexed in the moss
it surveyed the destruction, the remains of burning huts,
the dead and dying men. With its glassy eyes bright as
tungsten it saw the last flicker of life dissipating like
guttered candles. It saw glimmering, ghostlike bodies
slowly darkening into charcoal. It saw what this queer
precarious world would look like when it ended.

Lithe as a dancer it glided across the clearing to the
trailhead, stooping to pick up the dead scorpion. It
turned the insect over and over in its three-fingered,
prehensile hand, the lifeless creature's color fading to
black as death cooled it. The alien seemed puzzled, as if
it could not work out why this species man killed its

own kind *and* other kinds. Then it cocked its hairless bullet head and began to make a low humming sound that gradually modulated into an uncanny and dead accurate imitation of a human voice. Mac's voice.

"Dillon, over here," sounded the eerie, chilling mimicry as it replayed the scorpion incident.

Then the alien discarded the insect like a useless broken toy and strode across to the base of the tree from which it had descended. There it picked up its weapon —a short spear that it gripped like a rifle, another kind of homage. The weapon instantly changed color and keyed to the alien's skin, a merging of reptilian tones till the arm and the weapon were flesh of one flesh.

Instantly the creature turned and made for the trail where the men had disappeared. In seconds, with perfect simian dexterity, it had sprung to the lower branches of a tree, grasping the rough bark with its clawed, hammerlock fingers, pulling itself up through the branches with astonishing speed and agility. Then it leapt free into the air again, swinging exultantly from the crown of one tree to the next.

As it moved in the direction of the commando team it was actively stalking now; its passive observation was complete. In its wake the jungle froze in silence, as if every creature in the wild, weak or strong, suddenly considered itself fair game. What the moth knew, what the parrot knew, what the puma knew—at that moment the terror crossed all species, all except man. No wonder the temples were overgrown. No wonder the Mayan tribes had vanished without a trace. Man didn't even have the wit to run for cover.

EIGHT

JUST AHEAD OF the alien, below in the darkening shade, the team trudged along the bank of the lazily wandering stream, its pearly current illuminated here and there by slices of brilliant sunlight filtering through the foliage. A cloud of mosquitoes the size of bees dive-bombed them as they pushed forward along the marshy verge. Frustrated and tired they slapped and cursed their way, sweating like overworked slaves in the oppressive heat.

Around a bend where the water rippled over a rocky outcrop, a huge rotting tree lay across the group's path. Nerves were raw and spent all the way down the line. Blain was barely able to scramble over the obstacle, even with Mac assisting with the cumbersome machine gun.

"I've seen some badass bush before, but nothin' like this, man," Mac complained. Then, pulling a small silver flask from his shirt pocket, he offered Blain a slug of Tennessee mash.

"Little taste o' home, pardner?" he said with a wink.

Blain paused as he brushed the slugs and wood grubs off his pants. He nodded with exhausted enthusiasm, took the flask from his buddy, and hefted a swig.

"I hear you, bro'," he said, wiping his mouth with a grimy hand. "This is some shitpile. Makes Cambodia look like Kansas. Lose your way in here, man, you be in some kinda bad hurt." He returned the flask to Mac, who slipped it into his pocket. "You don't got much of that snake oil left, pal. We better save it case someone gets bit."

"Fuck the snake, man. Let him cop his own whiskey."

Laughing coarsely they bulldozed ahead, not wanting to waste the anesthetizing glow of the liquor. They were so tired they were punchy, yet still they wouldn't have minded a little action to get their blood moving. Few more dead guerrillas wouldn't hurt anyone. Few less bullets to haul out of the stinking place.

Dillon had fallen behind with Anna, who was stalling as much as she could. He watched ahead worriedly as the rest of the team outdistanced him. Then, adding to his problems, the rebel woman suddenly tripped on a root and stumbled to the ground, where she lay grunting, holding her knee.

Dillon reached down and dragged her up. "Shit, lady, come on," he demanded, his patience run dry.

As he hauled her up she managed to grab a handful of dirt and like a striking cobra flung it in his face, momentarily blinding him. As he coughed and rubbed his eyes she made a snatch for his rifle. But even as she got a grip on the butt of it, the barrel of another gun was shoved in her face.

It was Ramirez, calmly holding his weapon against her ear, his expression indicating that he'd like nothing better than to blow her head off.

"Don't even try it, sweetheart," he ordered her coldly.

Foiled but still defiant, Anna turned and obliged by moving forward up the trail, her shoulders lifted haughtily. As Dillon began to see again, blinking the tears away, Ramirez stared him down with a sneer.

"Maybe you should put her on a leash, man," he suggested with a guttural laugh. "If you can't handle her, just say the word." Like the others he kept gnawing away at Dillon, who was infuriated at the implication that he couldn't control a prisoner half his size. The black commander increased his pace to get away from the Chicano, catching up with Anna and turning her sharply by the elbow.

"Hey, bitch, don't try that again," he barked.

She looked back at him undaunted, staring at him mockingly with her head angled up, the proud rebel who would die for her cause without flinching. Perhaps she was as naive as she was tough, and perhaps she had no notion of how much she resembled her sister terrorists in Syria, in the Baader-Meinhof, wherever there was a righteous cause that demanded martyrs. No doubt she had clawed her way through the ranks of the rebel army by sheer courage and skill. In any case she was not to be underestimated. She broke away from Dillon's grasp and moved on, strictly obeying the rules of capture but giving him back nothing.

Not far above and just behind the last of the team, the alien had shifted to lower branches, silently swinging from tree to tree, keeping pace with the group and watching fascinated as they struggled up the primitive trail. It had also noted that the rebel prisoner was a different breed, though it couldn't really distinguish the gender difference from the political one.

To the alien the species appeared to break down into different subsets, like drones and workers. And the blond man with the massive shoulders was obviously the king, and the slighter figure with the deep black eyes was the tribe's magician. The alien understood all the dynamics. After all, it had seen the whole thing before.

For though no one among the commandos knew it yet, much rested with the Sioux warrior, and the thousand years of magic handed down through generations of his shaman forebears. Billy himself didn't know it. What the team did know was that the Indian had the best tracking nose of any soldier they'd ever encountered. Thus none of them hesitated to give him the lead. Just now he picked his way along the riverbank, his concentration rapt and keen, and that was all they ever needed of him. His face was fixed trancelike as he led his rattled comrades, and nobody knew how far he could see because all they wanted was to get through the next ten miles.

But the alien knew.

Behind Billy, Blain cradled his mini-cannon, now and then swinging the weapon from left to right across the field of view to make sure he had a good kill range. As he paused to adjust the belted loop of cartridges trailing from his backpack magazine, a mosquito landed on his face, lodging in the thick grease around his lips. Without interrupting his concentration he extended his tongue and drew the hapless bug into his mouth, then casually spat it out dead. The theory of natural selection triumphed once again.

Schaefer, next to Billy, was concentrating on the ground, kicking dried leaves aside and checking for hidden traps and natural obstacles. Every five minutes he double-checked the team's position and progress with map and compass, though the map had pretty much petered out by this point. They could only hope the unmarked trail would bring them out over the border.

Hawkins followed Blain, panting in the heavy humid air, the radio strapped across his back dragging him down like a load of bricks. Of course he could have abandoned the cumbersome equipment. No rule of combat demanded that he carry so much weight on a forced march, and besides, they wouldn't be needing it again anyway. They'd either make it to the LZ or they wouldn't, and there they could use the portable shortwave to signal the rescue choppers. But Hawkins was very attached to his radio. He was as proprietary about it as he used to be about his ghetto blaster back in the streets of South Boston.

The nerve-shot line of men began to ascend the east side of the riverbank, just before it narrowed into a vertical sheet of rock. As they climbed, Anna slipped in the muddy turf, falling again to her knees because she couldn't balance herself with her bound hands. Dillon, just behind her, prodded her with his rifle, a bit more roughly this time, forcing her to her feet. Again they fell behind a few meters more.

Billy, fronting the team, came to a small clearing above the crumbling slope of the riverbank. It was bordered on one side by towering fir trees, with the high canyon wall beyond turning rose and beaten gold in the westering sun. The upper branches were covered with a flock of bright blue birds squawking wildly, chasing

each other from branch to branch, feathers fanning in
rainbow hues.

Then, right in front of Billy, the birds' noises and
rustlings stopped for no apparent reason, as abruptly as
if some magic force had flicked a switch. The birds all
settled quietly along the branches, not even preening.
Billy stared up into the trees curiously, and when
Schaefer came over the bank into the clearing the Indian
held up three fingers, indicating possible ambush.
Schaefer waved a hand to the team as it reached the
plateau, and they froze in position.

Requiring no orders, they moved quietly and swiftly
into cover of the underbrush. Dillon dragged Anna
along with him, drawing his knife as they entered the
bush. Grasping the woman by her shirt collar he pushed
her to the ground, holding her face to the dirt and the
blade to her throat. Then he signaled Ramirez to approach.

"Take this and watch her," he ordered, passing the
hilt of the knife to the Chicano. Then Dillon disappeared deeper into the brush, determined to take command if there was danger.

Ramirez held the blade tight to Anna's jugular, but
his attention was diverted as he nervously scanned the
tall grass around him. Always on the alert for an opportunity, Anna used the momentary advantage to reach for
a root-burl lying loose on the ground beside her face.
She tucked it up next to her belly with her bound hands
and hoped it would prove useful.

While the others scouted around, Billy remained frozen in place, transfixed as he stared at the treeline. He
was aware again of a strange density in the air around
him, but couldn't locate any solid evidence to confirm

his suspicions—not a sound, not a shadow or even a rustle of leaves. The blue macaws sat row upon row in the fir trees, seeming to mock him. Yet he was certain something was out there, waiting, watching and burning with danger. On and on he stood motionless as a statue, till he seemed lost in a self-induced trance.

Schaefer, aware that his Indian tracker was going mystical on him, sidled up to Mac as if for the reassurance of a blunt, uncomplicated military animal. Mac chewed a dead cigar butt and watched the Sioux in the clearing with curiosity.

"What's got him so spooked?"

"Can't say yet," Schaefer replied without emotion. "But he's on to something. I've seen him do it before and I know enough not to get in his way."

After another couple of minutes Schaefer walked up softly behind Billy and stood watching as the lean Indian became more and more absorbed in his ritual. He reached half-consciously to his throat, grasping a thin rawhide cord secured around his neck. He ran two fingers under the cord, almost as if he was trying to breathe easier. In his head he imagined there was a small leather pouch attached to the rawhide, and Billy was reaching in and pulling out a pinch of dark powder, a powerful mix of mushroom buttons and moldy herbs that would deepen the trance. The whole time his eyes were wide, riveted on the canopy of leaves above him, pupils dilated and unblinking as he stared among the branches.

He was tapping another dimension now, the culmination of hundreds of years of inherited psychic sensitivity, Billy's birthright as the last of the shamans of his tribe. He had never been taught any of it. As he opened his mind now to vibrations from the unknown and unseen around him, as he zeroed in on the presence and drank its thoughts he was fully magic for the first time. What Schaefer had seen in him before was only a shadow of his transformation here. Billy had always ducked it in the past, or he shook it off like a dog shook water. Now he could not turn from it. He'd been waiting all his life to see as deep as this.

He was cast adrift in his tribe's collective memory, suffused with legends and ancient battles. He began to sway as he murmured an old Sioux chant, and though he could never have told what the words meant he saw the image clearly. The legend described a Herculean adversary who had come from the meadow beyond the sky, a god-creature of wrath who had murdered half of Billy's people. This was all a hundred generations ago. But the chant was very clear as it repeated over and over that the god-creature would return again. Billy quaked with fear as the chant locked in his throat. He could feel the breath of the ancient marauder, and the recognition sent shockwaves of horror through his soul.

Billy's eyes were wide and glassy now, as if he no longer needed them to see. Now he could focus directly on the alien's mind. He gathered all his strength till his ears rang with the beating of his blood. Now his own soul broke open like an extradimensional searchlight, and he scanned the jungle sky and intercepted the alien's thoughts, slicing into them like a laser.

But the intensity was tortuous, and Billy wavered and tried to pull back, his mind screaming from the stress of the trance. The ringing in his head accelerated now to a louder pitch as he began to lose his grip on the alien. He knew he had encountered a force stronger than all the hundred generations. Then his soul faltered, and his eyes rolled back in his head, and he collapsed in Schaefer's arms.

The major crouched gently, lowering Billy to the ground, the Indian's chest heaving as he gasped huge quantities of air. It was as if he hadn't breathed at all in the last five minutes. The sweat soaked out of him. His pulse beat furiously, his face beet red, and his temperature hovered at a hundred and three. He was like an overworked engine with burned-out gears and pistons, and for a moment Schaefer wasn't sure he could bring him back.

The major pulled a canteen from his belt and gushed water into Billy's mouth as if the choking would wake him up. Then he drenched a handkerchief and folded it over the Indian's eyes. After a couple of interminable minutes Billy blinked and stared into Schaefer's face. Still he seemed utterly dazed, as if some circuit in his brain had been snapped irrevocably.

"You okay, Billy?" Schaefer asked tensely.

For a moment, nothing. Then out of nowhere the macaws in the fir trees began to gabble and sing again. Schaefer looked up. Several were flying in whirling circles above the clearing, as if they were trying to charm Billy back.

"Yeah . . . yes, sir," Billy nodded feebly as he focused again on the real world. The color came up cooler in his face, and he struggled to sit. One hand gripped the major's arm as if he needed an anchor to keep from falling backward again.

"What the hell happened?" Schaefer asked in an awed whisper. "What did you see?"

"I don't know, sir," Billy replied in some bewilderment. "I had this dream. It was like a story somebody was trying to tell me. Only it was like I was supposed to know it already." He shook his head in confusion.

"What story?" demanded the major impatiently.

"The story of this place," said Billy with a strange smile. "The god-creature was here too." And before Schaefer could speak again Billy had held out an arm and pointed to the ground. Schaefer looked down and for the first time saw the faint trace of a broken wall, just a few stones mortared together amid the surrounding rubble. The side of one stone was incised with glyphs. Billy waved his arm in a casual circle, and suddenly Schaefer understood they were standing in the flattened ruin of a huge temple.

"God?" said the major with a faint distaste. "Whose god?"

"It's just the same," breathed Billy in a low voice, a look of astonishment in his eyes. "My people and these people—they both saw it. And they sing the same song too. That the god will return." There was no fear in Billy's voice just then. Perhaps that was the most fearful thing of all.

"Okay, Tonto, that's enough," retorted the major gruffly. "We better get moving. We got us a plane to catch."

And he stalked away to call up his men, trying to tell himself that the coast was clear and that it was all downhill from here. They were only three or four miles from pickup, and Billy had detected no enemy movement, whatever else was riddling his brain. Schaefer was used to the bird-dog frequency Billy hooked into. He respected it for purely radar purposes. He had no use for the metaphysical side of it.

As Schaefer left the clearing he looked back one last time and saw the Indian standing absolutely still. There was a blue macaw on Billy's shoulder as he stared transfixed at the broken temple wall. The Sioux shook his head with a great sorrow.

NINE

BESIDE THE ROCK pool where Dillon had turned over his combat knife to Ramirez, with orders to guard his unpredictable prisoner, the wiry Chicano had decided to replace the knife with his rifle. Blades reminded him too much of the small-time world of the barrio; he found more comfort in a loaded gun. With the gloat of a high school braggart leaving parking lot rubber with his Harley, he slouched his right shoulder to let the sling of his M-202 slip down his tattooed arm. His curled fingers caught the gun at its hand grip. Smirking with self-satisfaction, completely at one with the rifle, he extended the end of the cylinder and caressed Anna's tawny neck with a teasing threat. Then his attention went to his loaded belt to look for a loop in which to retire Dillon's inadequate knife.

In his macho dance he totally underestimated the girl's fast thinking and swift reflexes. The instant his eyes were averted she sprang from the ground in a flash. Twisting her bound arms in a furious contortion Houdini would have bowed to, she cracked Ramirez squarely over the right eye with the chunk of wood.

As his head split in two with pain, Ramirez saw

bright red lights and instinctively covered the eye with his hand. The arm with the rifle dangled useless. Again Anna took the moment's advantage, this time kicking him brutally in the groin, ramming his testicles right up to his intestines. Stunned, Ramirez's eyes gaped like a frog's as he doubled over in agony. He heaved like a drowning man going under, then choked out a single hollow cough that seemed to come from the pit of his stomach. The mute reaction wasn't a matter of stoic reserve, nor the mark of a soldier determined to salvage his pride in the face of defeat. It was rather a purely involuntary response, the kind a man makes when it hurts so much he's beyond screaming.

The next moment Ramirez collapsed to the ground and curled in a fetal position.

Anna Gonsalves didn't hang around to watch the special effects. She scrambled fast up the muddy slope beside the rock pool, parting her way through the thick border of broad-leaf ferns that followed up the ridge. Breaking out at the ridgeline, she hesitated in picking a direction. Though she knew this jungle better than all the commandos, she had never been this way, and any untracked place in the Usamacinta basin was a whole new game. She could only rely on luck and a certain instinctual sense, and she knew that no matter what she mustn't wander over the border. It was certain death for the likes of her, as much as it would save the U.S. team.

She started off into the jungle proper, feeling the wet heat the trees had captured. Behind her she could hear Ramirez, who had barely regained his speech. In a voice that rasped with the pain of his injured balls knifing through his body like high-voltage shocks, he managed to spit out a curse. "You motherfuckin' cunt," he hissed, "I'll slit your goddam throat."

But though it made him feel like a man again to say it he was still too paralyzed to stand, let alone give chase. The Chicano's wounds were a good deal worse than physical. The embarrassment and anger at being throttled by a woman—and one whose hands were tied to boot—would require a considerably longer recovery than a head gash and bruised gonads.

From here on Ramirez would despise the dark-eyed woman rebel with an intensity beyond reason. He knelt by the rock pool, propping himself on a fallen tree trunk, and seethed with a longing to carve out her heart with a slow machete. Yet even in the thick of the pain he had the presence of mind to shout to the others for help.

Schaefer, who was still trying to sort out Billy's story of the temple god—trying to *forget* it—heard Ramirez's cry and immediately dispatched Hawkins to check it out. "Move out, Irish. On the double."

Then the major turned on Dillon, who had just returned from a brisk reconnoiter of the surrounding bush in which he had encountered nothing. "Your girlfriend, no doubt," sneered Schaefer, refering to the obvious trouble that filtered through the trees with Ramirez's shout of alarm. "Didn't you hear me the first time, *Officer* Dillon," he growled sarcastically, pointing a threatening finger. *"You* babysit the bitch from now on. And don't fuckin' use my men again. Got it?"

Schaefer's patience for the boss with the desk job manner was over. Dillon glared back and said nothing, but his whole demeanor was chastened, as if he was registering a demerit.

* * *

Hawkins raced back through the jungle along the flank of the canyon wall and arrived at the rock pool just in time to see Anna hightailing it through the ferns at the top of the ridge. He bent down to Ramirez, still half-lying on the ground, one hand protectively cupping his crotch. Hawkins looked back and forth between his buddy and the disappearing hostage, torn between the two crises.

Ramirez looked up, his eyes still watering from the pain. He sensed the Irishman's indecisiveness. "I'm okay," he gasped. "Just get that bitch," he gritted through clenched teeth, as if the outcome of an entire war depended on bringing her in.

Hawkins tore off up the ridge after Anna, probably no more than a hundred paces behind her but with no certain knowledge of which direction she'd taken. It was her jungle, not his. Besides, Irish had less experience in the field than the rest of the commando team, usually because he was stuck in one spot trying to put together a radio out of old rusty flashlights.

Meanwhile, even with her hands still bound, Anna —fit as a gymnast—darted rabbitlike around trees and ducked like a jackal through the underbrush. She was so single-minded about escaping she forgot her never-quite-mastered fear of prowling pumas and the deadly vipers slithering underfoot that she could easily, in her rush, disturb. She'd been brought up in the capital city, and her great guerrilla triumphs had involved the planting of bombs in government buildings and embassies. She had proudly, tenaciously, marched with her unit to the jungle hideout to prepare for the great offensive, but something in her had never lost the childhood fear of the wild. Her youth in the city had been pampered by nuns and European governesses. The jungle, though only miles away, was the other side of the world.

If she had known what *was* tracking her, the thoughts of snakes and wildcats would have seemed innocent as a child's dreams.

For when Anna overcame Ramirez only minutes before, the alien had been crouching in the upper branches of a mahogany tree towering above the rock pool. It had sensed, and in its way relished, every detail of the skirmish between the two. Curious and obsessed, it watched Ramirez clutch his groin, instinctively understanding who was the loser, who the winner. It watched the rebel woman clamber away up the ridge with a sense of triumph spilling over from its own soul. It suddenly longed for a victory of its own, so it could fly with the winner and kill the winner and have it all.

Exultantly transforming itself from observer mode to predator mode, it quickly searched the surrounding sky till it settled on a hawk sailing gracefully by, its wings held perfectly still while the heat-soaked air currents wafted it like a billowing schooner. The unearthly intruder followed the bird's flight with its heat vision. Then, with its sixth-sense power of capture, it zeroed in on the hawk's essence, its mind steering the bird toward it like some remote-controlled toy. The hawk's soul was lost to the alien, possessed like a zombie.

For this was the effortless power the alien found it had over every creature it encountered on the host planet—every one, that is, but man. It could kill a man but not take him over—could dissect him down to the cell structure, but not inhabit him body and soul. Perhaps it was the elusive matter of the soul that made man impenetrable to the alien—man the justice-giver, man the idea-maker. Something in any case that the alien lacked, and all the more reason to destroy the species utterly if there was no other way of possessing it.

Wings frozen, the hawk dropped helplessly from the air, and the alien snatched it out of the sky with an outstretched hand. It pulled the bird close and held it gently in both three-fingered hands, fanning the white neck feathers where the quivering bird lay paralyzed. Then the alien bent its head down and almost seemed to nuzzle the bird, purring as if to calm it—till the stunning transformation occurred. First the alien's skin swirled with all the mottled autumn shades, hues blending and churning like a kaleidoscope till it settled on the exact slate gray of the bird's feathers. Then its lizardlike skin swirled down and its form melted and compressed and took the hawk's shape. When it was an exact clone of the animal it dropped the limp hawk from its talons, letting it fall to be consumed by predators of its own.

An instant later the reincarnated hawk flapped its wings as if it had just awakened to a new day. Its razor talons released their viselike grip on the topmost branch. Soaring into the air it set off up the ridge after Anna and Hawkins. Unlike the true hawk, which drifted in wide dreamlike circles, the alien slapped the air with a surge of power as it sped over the trees, drinking in the species at the peak of force, in a wild drunken thirst for prey. With the easy edge of a bird in a race with the earthbound it sailed above its prey, catching the girl's pace but then outdistancing her by a hundred yards and lazily combing back in a hawk's pure circle.

As Anna struggled to stay ahead of Hawkins she glanced back anxiously every few seconds. The sounds of snapping twigs and the rush of leaves grew louder as he closed in on her. Though he was encumbered by the radio strapped to his back and the M-202 slung over his shoulder, Irish was in superb condition and steamrollered after the rebel woman with relentless stamina. Because she was so panicked her trail was a snap to follow. Even if he'd had to move slower there was never any question about laying aside the radio. It went where Hawkins went—period.

When Anna broke through the dense trees onto the canyon rim and into a more navigable grove of ferns, she still had a thirty-meter lead but was heaving from exhaustion. Moments later she came to a natural clearing, a long unbroken alley between rows of tall bamboo trees that grew in such perfect rank they looked planted. Taking advantage of the opening she sprinted down the alley as fast as she could, surging forward with a last throb of energy as if she were crossing a finish line.

Hawkins drove down hard on her now and closed the gap. He bore down like a madman along the bamboo alley, the great weight on his back roaring him forward on the slight downhill slope. Anna was only ten feet in front of him. Five feet. Then she slipped a half inch as she trod over a rotting melon, and the instant's hesitation gave Irish his chance. He lunged out as he overtook her, knocking her to the ground. Immediately he had his rifle cocked and pinned her neck to the ground. Then he roughly rolled her over with his foot and placed the barrel tight between her eyes.

Anna's eyes darted back and forth in panic, staring into the threatening black hole of the rifle and combing the pitiless jungle as she frantically weighed her alternatives. Out of the corner of one eye she caught a glimpse of furious upheaval farther down the alley. Hawkins's back was turned so he couldn't see it. Anna assumed with a bitter sinking of the heart that it was another of the commandos catching up with them. So flight was out of the question. Anna stared up the barrel at the cold-eyed Irishman, wondering what sort of tack she ought to take—pleading, seduction, screaming, sobbing. Once again she darted a glance down the alley to see which of the others had joined them, hoping it might be the weak-hearted black man—

And suddenly, there in the low grass about twenty yards away, was the alien, standing clear, for the first time making no attempt to disguise itself from view. It had discarded its hawk disguise and returned to its normal humanoid form—a creature who seemed from Anna's vantage to be nearly as tall as the trees. Its cobra skin swirled with color. Its masklike face appeared to be peeling away from its great golden honeycomb eyes. It waved its weapon above its head in silent communion with the warrior stars of deep space. Its Darwinian battle with an equal was engaged at last.

The sight of it was so horrifying that Anna nearly blacked out. Her brute survivor's instinct was the only thing that kept her sane, and the impact of the monster was such as to temporarily erase her blood rivalry with the soldiers. In an instant man against man had turned to man against devil. Her eyes went wide with shock, and her mouth fell slack. She tried to whimper a warning to the Irishman. Hawkins figured she was scared he'd shoot her.

"Listen, sweetass," he said, "don't give us any more shit, okay? You're not dead yet, and neither are we. Let's keep it that way, huh?"

She didn't hear a word of it as she limply held out a hand, pointing down the bamboo alley at the alien as it flared its weapon to life. "Look . . . look out . . . behind you," she gasped in breathless Spanish.

Hawkins assumed she was pulling a stunt to divert his attention, yet he saw the real terror in her eyes and heard the shiver in her halting tone. He turned slightly to glance over his shoulder while still covering the girl. As he did so he saw a weird blur, the mottled outline of the creature looming toward them, its saber wheeling in the air above its head.

It seemed as if the entire wall of the jungle were caving in as the alien covered the distance like a bolt of lightning. Anna and Hawkins froze at the sight and instinctively shrank toward each other. But there was no real time to react in thought, let alone in action, though Hawkins managed to fire one lonely misguided bullet which whizzed off uselessly into the seething sky. It was to be his final defense.

In a second the alien's weapon ripped through Hawkins's throat and shot out the other side. The impact sent the Irishman hurling backward till he landed with a sickening crash in the undergrowth thirty feet away. Anna was left prostrate on the ground, covered with the commando's blood.

Shaking uncontrollably, she crawled on her hands and knees to the side of the alley and crouched in a heap against a bamboo trunk, sobbing like a lost child. She started biting the ends of her fingers like a psychotic, her face ghost white as she stared at the shredded track of turf where Hawkin's body had shot across the ground.

She began to pray, after a fashion. The words

drooled out of her and made no sense, but the sound was the sound she'd made in the convent, murmuring among the nuns twenty years ago. Her white-dress first communion god seemed very far away, but it was the only god she knew.

Behind the cover of the bushes where Hawkins had disappeared, arms and legs flailing like a broken puppet, head barely hanging from his body by shreds of torn cartilege, the alien dispassionately hooked its third spurred finger into the Irishman's leg like a meat hook. Then it dragged the body off through the jungle, limp as a fallen deer.

Anna had retreated even further now into a sort of catatonia and didn't notice anything. If only she could have recovered her hunger for freedom she would've been able to run away scot-free. Now was her chance. The alien appeared to be content with a single trophy at a time, as if it needed to focus its whole mind on a microscopic examination of one pure specimen. Anna could have fled it all like a fevered tropical nightmare, emerging once again to the rational bombs and espionage of the disintegrating capital. Yet she'd been pitched too far off balance by the horror she'd witnessed. It wouldn't go away and wouldn't behave like a dream, and she lay in a heap against the tree trunk, trembling as if she would never wake.

TEN

IN THE CROOK of the sunset canyon below, the rest of the men had gathered at Schaefer's signal. They waited for Ramirez and Hawkins, skittish as corraled horses getting wind of a stalking mountain lion. They smoked black Panama cigarettes to the knuckle and scrutinized the shadowing jungle with trigger-happy reflexes. Each was anxious and worried for the two men still out there, especially after hearing the lone gunshot. As the silence deepened after the echo died, the one shot seemed like an awful omen, like a bad game of Russian roulette.

Blain cradled his grenade launcher as affectionately as a first-born son. "One o' them monkeys shows his face and I'll send him back to his dead grandmother," he cracked gruffly out of the side of his mouth to Mac. It seemed like such an empty threat in a place where nothing human moved and nothing so simple as a war played out. But the bluff cliché was not what mattered here. It was as if the mere words—any words—would break up the heavy cloud hanging over the men.

Mac chuckled briefly. "Can I kill the other grand-mother?" It was good to lighten the intensity even for a second.

Schaefer, huddled with Billy, was trying to make sense of the psychic whirlwind from which the Sioux had just emerged. The major, a hard-core Baptist-raised nonbeliever in Santa Claus and a three-dimensional fan from head to toe, was wary of Billy's dream state. Yet from the ditches of Da Nang to the smithereens of Cambodia he had never encountered the kind of barbaric cruelty he'd uncovered in the wake of the downed chopper. Billy might be talking like a nut case, Schaefer thought, but he also knew well that the kid had never steered him off-target—not once. So the major tried his best to pry open his mind to the far-out possibilities Billy was intimating.

"Lemme get this straight," Dutch said slowly, his brow furrowed with skepticism. "You say you saw God, only he looked like some kinda space monster?"

Billy stood his ground, absolutely centered by his vision. "That's one way to put it, sir."

"What the hell is this, *The Twilight Zone?* I got enough trouble just gettin' through this fuckin' jungle alive."

But Billy's insight had been so crystal clear, his conviction so solid, he realized there wasn't a minute to waste on an introductory course in psychic awareness. One of the reasons he'd been able to tune in so acutely to the intruder's thoughts was that the alien had begun to focus more individually on the men as it systematically took and dissected them. Right away it had sought to share something with the Indian, recognizing in him a kindred spirit. So Billy had the most highly developed vision of the alien's mission, and he knew he simply had to convince the major to trust him.

"Sir, you gotta believe me," he almost pleaded.

"We're in terrible danger. There's a force out there . . . we'll call it a creature. It's already killed the three guys back at the chopper. I don't even know if we can stop it. But it's after us now, I'm sure of it. There's no time to explain how I know. But I swear, Major, trust me on this one. I wish I was wrong but I'm not. If I'm wrong I'll turn in my stripes and sell Injun rugs on Route Eighty—that is, if we ever get outa here alive." He looked expectantly at Schaefer, but with the utter calm of a man touched by divine vastness.

"Christ, Billy," Schaefer groaned, shaking his head in bewilderment. But he knew a decision had to be made that instant. "All right, we got no other choice but to keep movin' double time. Whatever it is out there, I'm not gonna sit and wait for the autopsy—especially mine. You lead the way, same as always. But don't tell none of the others about this monster business."

Schaefer stood up decisively and whistled to the others: "Okay, we move out!"

Just as he called the order Ramirez limped into the clearing, blood caked on his forehead, the dried red streaks fanning out across his cheek like warpaint. He stood like a specter, swaying as if he would faint at any moment.

Blain saw him first. With typical drop-dead bluntness he exclaimed, "Jesus, man, you look like fuckin' Dracula."

The rest turned as Blain spoke, crouching and ready to return fire as Ramirez gasped out his story. "The girl —she got away," he explained breathlessly. "Hawkins followed her up the canyon, but then right after that I heard a shot. So I came back here to get you guys. We gotta go find them."

As Ramirez spoke, Billy was already hacking through a mass of ferns on the ridge slope, the most direct route to Hawkins and the girl. The Indian knew from the sound of the gunshot exactly which way to steer. The plan to head out had now been abandoned as quick as the order had been given, simply because one of their own was in trouble. Mac helped Ramirez along as the others climbed the ridge, moving out in an offense/defense pattern, combing every inch of jungle with weapons cocked as they pushed forward.

It was scarcely a couple of minutes before they broke through the last of the ferns to the canyon rim where Anna had passed and on into the long moss-covered alley, the murder site still ripe and raw with the latest desecration. Billy was the first to reach the emotionally spent girl, but the others quickly caught up with him. The six commandos stood in a semicircle round the cowering Anna, each wrestling with a dread that only seemed to grow more nightmarish, and these were men who spent their lives strangling the guts out of nightmares. Anna's blood-splattered face was glazed with terror, her eyes vacant, her pupils dilated black as onyx, as if she had just seen Satan himself. She wasn't even aware of the commandos' presence.

Dillon knelt down and shook her shoulder gently. "Hey . . . hey, what the hell happened?" he demanded, louder and louder, trying to revive her. But it was useless. She curled there quivering, lost in her nightmare, stubborn almost, as if it would be more terrible to wake and have to tell it. Then Dillon wiped some of the blood from her face with the back of his hand and carefully turned her head looking for a wound. There was none.

"I don't think it's her blood," he announced in a slightly dazed voice.

Schaefer looked grim. "Dillon, you stay with her," he said flatly, taking control, totally ignoring rank. "All right, let's look around," he ordered, turning to the remaining soldiers. Schaefer's natural leadership role was surfacing strong and clear in the grip of danger. Hierarchy meant little in the kind of crisis that whittled men down to the soul. In any case Dillon was too scared to argue.

Already Billy had been scouting the immediate area and stumbled on Hawkins's weapon and radio. He trotted back to the others hauling the blood-splattered equipment and dumped it unceremoniously on the ground.

"Major, you better check this stuff out," said the Indian urgently.

"Hawkins?" Schaefer questioned, nodding toward the broken gear and not really needing an answer.

"I think so," Billy replied, shying ever so slightly from the truth.

"Let's get on it!" And they all fanned out, Ramirez quickly picking up the torn track of mossy turf across the alley and the crushed section of underbrush through which Hawkins's body smashed till it slammed against a bamboo trunk. Climbing through the broken brambles, his head and balls still throbbing, Ramirez walked straight into a pile of bloody human entrails oozing against the base of the tree. Ravenous flies had already zeroed in on the meal and swarmed in a frenzy around the slick red pool.

Schaefer was right behind the Chicano and stared down at the bloody heap, stunned all over again. "What in God's name . . ." he muttered bitterly, thinking with a sudden chill how terribly cruel a godless world could be. And even though he'd always supposed he believed in nothing, he prayed just then for something to help them. Anything.

"I think it's Hawkins, Major," Billy offered.

"Then where the hell is his body?" Schaefer demanded.

Billy pointed to the ground a few feet away. "Tracks, Major," he said. Heading off into the jungle were three-toed footprints almost eighteen inches long. A deep hole punctured the ground at the back of each print from the powerful hooked spurs that protruded from the alien's heels. Schaefer swallowed hard, a sick feeling rising in his stomach. At that moment he realized he could no longer deny the evidence. And Billy was definitely not on his way to selling rugs in Louisiana.

"What the fuck?" said Blain, incredulous as he stared down at the prints. "Even these fuckin' contras don't got Russian shoes with prints like that. That ain't no guerrilla. That ain't even . . ." And the man went speechless, who had always before kept the words flowing, even when the bullets were zinging overhead.

Schaefer took up where Blain left off. "Not even human," he said soberly. "Not even an animal."

"Then what?" whispered Blain.

"Pal, we don't even got a name for it. *That's* how bad it is."

Without a word they began to follow the tracks until they reached a point hardly fifty yards from the hideous pool of guts—where the footprints simply stopped, as if whatever made them had vanished into thin air again or taken to the sky.

Schaefer considered the situation for a second. "Okay, back to the girl. She's our only hope for an answer."

As the commandos marched back to where the rebel woman was being watched by Dillon, she was beginning to come around. A slight moaning issued from her lips, as if she were begging her way back to reality. As Dillon bathed her lips with water from his canteen, the major approached and stood just a few feet from her, hands on his hips. She looked up at Schaefer and struggled to focus as he towered above her, his massive muscular frame casting a shadow that blocked her whole body from the late orange sun. She seemed grateful for the shade, but otherwise she looked pitiful. The spark and fury, the whole rebel spirit, had been knocked out of her forever.

Schaefer realized how threatening he must look and so squatted next to her and spoke soothingly. In gentle Spanish he tried to evoke a response. He took up her hand in a gesture of truce. "My man caught up with you, didn't he?" he said. "Then something happened. Who attacked you? How'd this blood get on you?"

Anna looked at the major, baffled and teary-eyed. For the first time since the attack she began to form words, barely recognizable, but nonetheless she was talking at last. "The . . . the whole jungle . . . it came alive," she stumbled. "More than a jaguar—more than all the snakes. It ripped him open and dragged him . . . over there." And she pointed to the crushed bushes, the spot where Hawkins's body had flown like a broken puppet.

The rest of the men had been standing quietly a few feet away. "Christ, she don't make any sense," Dillon broke in. "It's the damn guerrillas, and she knows it. All we gotta do is go in there and grab 'em. Let's go."

Ramirez, searching desperately for a logical explanation, frightened of the truth, quickly patched together a story. "Coupla monkeys been trailing us all the way from the camp, Major," he said with bold assurance. "Billy heard 'em. *She* musta set us up and then ran for it," he reasoned, pointing at the shocked girl. "They were waitin' all this time. I shoulda wasted the bitch when I had the chance," he snarled.

Schaefer looked at Hawkins's blood-stained gun and radio, then back to Anna, sorting through the sketchy evidence, trying to make it fit anything but Billy's version.

"Then why didn't they take the radio and his gun?" he asked brutally, puncturing the first hole in Ramirez's story. "And why didn't she escape?" he added, nodding to Anna. "If they fuckin' came to rescue her, how come they forgot her?"

No response. Everyone was dumbstruck and squirming with discomfort. Then Billy broke the silence. "It's the same thing happened to Davis," he announced grimly. The air of certainty in his voice was unmistakable.

Schaefer was suddenly red with rage, impatient and adamant. He made his intentions savagely clear. "I want Hawkins *found,*" he ordered, looking around at the others. "Sweep pattern and double back. Fifty meters," he barked, indicating the range of jungle he wanted scoured by the inch. He slammed his fist in his hand ready to burst with frustration.

The soldiers spread into the darkening jungle, turning it inside out, bush by bush, deadfall by deadfall. High in the bowl of the canyon Schaefer came to a tall sycamore with a heavy carpet of vibrant green moss growing lush around its base. His keen eye was drawn to a bril-

liant scarlet spot, about four inches across, which stood
out in vivid contrast to the green. The major crouched
and studied the dark red mark, then touched it with the
tip of his forefinger and felt the wet slick of it.

"Blood," he said blankly to himself, his shoulders
sinking slightly as if with the weight of grief to come.
Even as he spoke a drop of the red liquid landed in the
center of the stain with a dull plop. He looked up reluc-
tantly, clenching his jaw in anticipation of the new horror. Above him in the dense foliage he saw a spattering
of more red drops dripping slowly from leaf to leaf from
high in the upper branches. The dry tawny sycamore
leaves clattered against each other with a mournful
sound.

Then he saw it, hanging so high it was nearly at the
top of the tree. Suspended from the ankles much in the
way Davis's crew had been, Hawkins's body swayed
like a grisly pennant, hideously displayed, his chest
ripped open and emptied of its organs. Above the normal hum of the jungle the only intruding sound was the
screeching of a couple of vultures as they fought over
rights to the flesh. The body was trussed like an animal
strung up to dry in the sun, and the slight upper breezes
gentled it slowly back and forth, the eerie movement
giving the hideous illusion of life in death. And nothing
wept and nothing cried out. For all its awfulness it was
death the same as ever. The choked and meaningless
jungle didn't even notice.

Unblinking, Schaefer stared up at the gruesome
sight. Without taking his eyes off the mangled body of
the Irishman he gave out with his low whistle, summoning the rest of the team to his side. There was something
hopeless in the whistle, somber as plain chant. There

was no question that he was summoning them to death.

The major was too absorbed to notice Blain arrive first, so the burly commando said nothing and merely followed the fix of Schaefer's eyes. Even such a jaded veteran as Blain, witness and sometime participant in acts of barbaric cruelty, was stunned into silence. Blain's jaws hadn't been emptied of tobacco juice since he shoved the first plug in his mouth at twelve years old—until now, that is. His mouth fell open as he gasped and the spongy rancid pulp spilled out, glanced off his belt buckle and landed in the dirt, followed by a thick stream of brackish spit veined with yellow-brown that drooled helplessly down his chin. He wiped his mouth with the back of his grimy sleeve, then instinctively and without a word pulled his rifle to his shoulder, released the safety catch and faced the savage jungle as if it was another planet.

For the Irishman was the first member of the team killed in action in the whole seven years they'd been operating as a unit. Davis and his crew had been mates to several of the commandos in one mission or another, but they weren't part of the brotherhood of six. Hawkins was one of their own. Until this moment they were in some real way invincible. And now there was a break in the line, and anything could happen.

ELEVEN

As THE OTHER commandos gathered, Blain bit off another inch of sticky plug and moved out impulsively, scanning the tangled jungle with his rifle, desperate to take revenge. The whole time he was sputtering to himself about the bastard rebels he planned to skewer on his machete and send to hell for the barbecue. Anyone and anything in his path would be dead meat, he promised Hawkins silently. Yet even in his rage he paid acute attention to any tip-offs the jungle might offer of enemy presence—a snapping twig, the glint of a gun chamber between the branches of a rubber tree.

A minute later he was obliged by a rustling deep in the bushes ten yards ahead. Carefully, silently, he pulled the rifle sight to his eyes and focused the crosshairs in the direction of the noise. "C'mon ya shit-eatin' mothas," he hissed with a mad grin, anticipating revenge. "Lemme see your fuckfaces so I can fill 'em full o' holes!" And he began to squeeze slowly on the trigger, waiting in a kind of rapture for the right moment.

He expected a terrorist—maybe two, maybe more. It didn't matter. A dozen would suit him just fine. He'd let go the whole round in a second and make garbage of all of them. The sound grew more distinct, and Blain held his breath to steady his aim.

"C'mon fuckers . . . c'mon right in," he whispered. "Ol' painless ain't got no patience."

Suddenly sounds of a charge—and a small tapir burst through the leaves, whinnying with its ears back as it scampered across the clearing and dived through the high canyon grass. Blain winced, then exhaled in deflated surprise as the animal disappeared from sight. "Shit!" he cursed, exasperated. His body, tensed from head to toe in hyperalertness, relaxed at the sight of the animal, going almost limp from the anticlimax.

But just as he permitted his senses to rest and go off alert he felt a curious piercing burn across his shoulders. And echoing like a mockery in his ears he could hear Hawkins's voice, sounding almost as if it were underwater: "Hey, Blain, you ever heard of a toothbrush?" Blain looked down bewildered in the direction of the sting, and he saw a gout of blood erupting from a tear in his shirt.

He spun around, raising his rifle a second too late, only to be greeted by the alien's spear streaking toward him like a guided missile. The creature attacked in its own concept of time, a blurred streak inhumanly fast, measured by the millisecond. The razor sharp weapon entered Blain's back at the base of the spine, ripping through the spinal column with a force so awesome it cut through bone and burst out through his chest. He just had time to let out a half-scream that drowned out all the rest of the jungle, the screeching parrots and blue-hair monkeys, the million cicadas whizzing their legs.

Grotesquely, the tip of the alien spearhead pierced

Blain's heart and rocketed it out of the body, the organ attached to the tip like a macabre trophy. A hundred Mayan priests sighed in their temple graves. Then the deadly weapon slammed into the side of a bamboo tree, and the heart exploded in a bloody pulp that clung to the bark, the veiny red flesh as weird as an alien presence itself. Blain's body, which stood dead on its feet for seconds that would have seemed like hours to an observer, at last keeled over on the ground. The cavernous hole through Blain's chest was big enough for the tapir to crawl through.

Close by, Mac heard the short burst of Blain's wail and scrambled up the canyon toward the sound. As he charged into the clearing where Blain had stood moments before he saw nothing but a newly roughed-up track of dirt; then beyond, the alien's spear still vibrating from the impact with the tree. With his M-22 readied, Mac stalked closer in time to hear a strange wet sucking sound like a famished peasant pulling a bowl of soup to his lips.

He stopped for a second and listened, bewildered, then pushed aside a red fern leaf and saw the retreat of the mighty, two-legged creature—not ape, not man, but warrior without a doubt—as it raced off into the trees. Laying on the ground just inches away was the shell of Blain's body. Mac looked down and saw his partner's deflated corpse emptied of its organs, a kidney and a few feet of intestines strewn nearby, dropped accidentally by the monster as it flashed away.

The commando choked and could feel the banana he'd eaten before the rebel attack erupt into his mouth. He turned his head aside and blew out the sticky, half-digested yellow mass, then shook his head and sobbed out loud, wiping his stinging eyes in disbelief.

Yet he quelled his grief quickly in favor of a passion for revenge. He pulled his wits together, drew his rifle to his chest and aimed nakedly in the direction in which the alien had fled. As he blasted into the trees he shouted a wild and primitive war call—not a cry he'd learned in basic training, but one that came directly from the soul, the unconsolable wail of agony when a man loses a brother.

He emptied the entire magazine at his waist before thinking to call out to the others. But it didn't matter. Every living thing within a radius of two miles heard Mac's raw scream and the explosion of gunfire. Immediately the commandos were on their way, tearing through the brush in a kind of frenzy, as if they barely had a second now to tie a tourniquet on this nightmare.

When Mac's ammunition was exhausted he reached down and grabbed up his buddy's rifle, which had snagged on a bramble during the havoc. Once more he poured the ammunition into the black-green vegetation, riddling the trunks of trees and scattering nests and bursting seed pods, as if the jungle itself must die for this one. His glazed saucer eyes were possessed as he swept the gun back and forth across the path. Whatever reserves a man can muster, Mac burned now with a white fire, then summoned more to burn again. In his crazed state now he would happily level the entire country and all the rotten dictatorships bordering it if necessary, anything to wipe out the wrongness responsible for his best buddy's murder.

The other commandos were zeroing in on the site one by one, erupting out of the choking brush.

"What the hell's goin' on," Ramirez bawled to Mac,

shouting to compete with the deafening crack of bullets ripping from Blain's rifle.

Mac screamed back without a second's holding fire. "It got Blain!" he cried. "Ran that way!" And he let off another stream of bullets into the splintered grove of bamboo to point the way.

"Lemme give you a little light," Ramirez hissed with an edge of black humor as he released his grenade launcher and *whumped* two volleys into the jungle. Seconds later a pair of deafening explosions sent fragments of dirt and leaves and sticks everywhere, knocking birds from the air as the canyon roared with a phosphorous light. Then the blinding chaos was followed by the stunned silence of aftershock, as if the whole world had paused for a breath of grief.

The alien, racing among the trees, stopped in its tracks as the white flash from the grenade explosion short-circuited its heat-seeking vision, momentarily paralyzing it. As it froze in a crouch, a shard of shrapnel zinged through the air and managed to lodge in its thick-hided shoulder. It barely felt the merest twinge of pain, but the gash was deep enough to cause a glob of blood—a thick, translucent, amber jelly—to splash on the leaves of a kingfire bush.

The group of men, now including Schaefer and finally Dillon dragging Anna along behind, stood wide-eyed in the clearing, ears ringing painfully as they waited for the jungle to settle. For a moment the only movement was the pale blue smoke wafting from the end of Mac's rifle. And every one of them looked as if he hadn't a clue where to go from here. Their dozen wars suddenly amounted to nothing, and their massive kills and their awesome bravery and luck were as meaningless as the random swarms of bees that floated like liquid gunfire in the deep of the woods.

Anna suddenly broke free from Dillon's clench on her arm and wobbled over to Blain's body as if she were drawn by a kind of spell. As she looked down at the mangled flesh her eyes glazed over in renewed terror. But this time she didn't go rigid with shock as she did at Hawkins's run-in with fate. Schaefer watched her carefully, knowing the girl's recollections and Mac's report might shed some light on the workings of the enemy's mind. As Anna stared transfixed in horror the major glanced between the two witnesses, impatient for some answers.

Mac spoke first. "I . . . I saw it," he stammered.

"What? Saw what?"

"I saw it," he repeated dully. "Fuckin' thing . . ." And his voice trailed away as if there were no more words to describe it.

Then Mac and Anna, both looking down at the body, simultaneously raised their heads. They locked eyes in recognition, as if they shared a common secret. The same thing had cut out both their tongues.

Schaefer's patience was spent. He turned to Mac and shouted. "Mac! Mac! Look at me, goddam it!"

The brute soldier stared ahead dumbly, his face numb with shock. He'd shot all his bullets. His power was over, and his rage was useless.

"Who did this?" Schaefer demanded, shaking him by the shoulders angrily.

Suddenly Mac was furious too, as he groped his way out of his trance, furious because he had no explanation. "I don't know what the fuck did it," he said with disgust. "Somethin' terrible . . . big like a gorilla, only it didn't have no hair. I saw it, Major, I saw it," he insisted almost pathetically, as if fearful no one would believe him.

As Mac was struggling to describe the alien, Ramirez, who'd been nosing around the immediate area, came running back to the dwindling group.

"Nothing, Major. Not a fuckin' trace," he reported in a rage of frustration. "Like they all disappeared in a hole in the ground."

The stunned and bewildered commandos instinctively moved closer to Schaefer, gathering round him as if to draw comfort and direction from their leader. Schaefer looked up at the yellowing sky now beginning to roll with heavy dark clouds, the day fading into a dusk that would grow no cooler, only wilder.

"We're losing the light," he said quietly. "I want a defensive position set up at the top of the ridge. Empty all your pockets. We're gonna need everything we got."

Mac, agitated to such a pitch that he growled like a cornered puma, forced himself to get calm again, at least enough to get back to business. "Yes, sir," he replied vigorously to Schaefer, relieved to dive into a project and distract himself from his grief and rage over Blain.

Even Schaefer was nervous, though. He realized this elusive enemy was a tactical magician with tricks up its sleeve they hadn't even dreamed of. Shreds of evidence were slowly, if vaguely, piecing together, confirming Billy's far-out notion that some kind of unearthly killer was on the loose. As the jungle grew swathed in shades of purple the major knew his team would be ever more vulnerable to the mysterious predator who was picking his men off one by one.

And the most unsettling thing was this: Schaefer had always been able to understand before exactly why an enemy hated him. They shared their opposite sides of a war and fought as best they could as heroes. Here he was sure of nothing whatsoever. The enemy came from nowhere, and it had no army and it had no country and it had no creed and it had no mercy.

Urgent as the time was, Schaefer felt compelled to allow Blain a last dignity, however makeshift, before setting up camp for the night. "Put him in his poncho liner for now," said the major, pointing toward the ravaged body. "We'll bury him in the morning."

"*I'll* take him," Mac said urgently, determined to cover his buddy even in death.

And while Mac attended to the cerements, the rest of the commandos climbed the steep canyon to the campsite Schaefer had chosen. Anna, her eyes drawn to a nearby bush, wandered slightly away from the group unnoticed by the others. They all understood she was too freaked out to flee. But this was no attempt to escape. She had noticed the queer glimmering spot of orange among the leaves. As she approached the bushes she reached out, her fingers hovering over the leaves where the alien's blood gleamed, its color and irridescence like a distillation of all the jungle's mottled orchid hues.

Tentatively she touched a fingertip to the saplike glob, then drew her hand close to her eyes and examined a drop of it as curiously and innocently as a child pinching the wings of its first butterfly. Anna had not quite returned to the real world. Though functional again, she had preserved some part of herself in a distant and safe buffer zone in her mind, soothing as a fairy tale. She was insulated now from the full screaming terror she'd witnessed earlier, and her fascination with the amber depths of the alien's crystalline blood was a way of pretending the nightmare never happened.

As she vacantly studied the odd substance, sniffing it delicately, Dillon came up behind her. She looked up with a smile as he motioned her to return with him. Shrugging like a child Anna passively obeyed, absentmindedly wiping her sticky fingers on her fatigue pants.

Then Dillon and the newly docile Anna—the antithesis now of the fiery Amazon who'd been taken at the guerrilla camp—walked silently back up the slope to the others. The commandos had begun to establish their defensive camp in a dense grove of firs that abutted a solid wall of canyon rock. They had already dug makeshift foxholes, and Ramirez and Billy and Mac were kneeling in theirs, weapons cocked and ready.

Their sweaty fatigues were well suited to the high-country surroundings, the greens and browns fading with the daylight, the dark tones all merged in a way that seemed almost magically unified—except that by comparison the alien's capacity for camouflage was lightyears ahead.

Dillon helped Anna step into a shallow foxhole where she huddled in her dreamlike state, rocking in a slow and methodical way like a mental patient on high-dose salts. Now and then she looked down at the alien bloodstain, which glowed sweetly in the gathering dark with a faint orange luminosity. Slowly she moved a hand toward the spot and stroked it lightly, then caught her breath with a shiver, as if a memory of the brutal attack on Hawkins had rushed to the front of her mind. Then the next stroke seemed to calm her down, and she fell into a peaceful doze.

Nearby Mac was stringing a trip wire low to the

ground, covering it with leaves and grass. After completing a wide circle maybe fifty feet across, till there wasn't a single break surrounding the site, he moved into camp and reported to Schaefer.

"We got most of the flares set up," he said. "And two claymores just outside. Nothin's comin' close without trippin' on somethin'."

"Good work, Sergeant," Schaefer acknowledged curtly, his mind trying to process a hundred details. Then, suddenly sensitive to the bond that lay broken between Blain and Mac, he added softly, "I'm sorry, Bull. It's never easy. He was a good man."

"I never had no brother. He was it," Mac replied simply, almost matter-of-factly, his lips tightened as if to contain his emotions.

Then he walked back over to the poncho containing Blain's body where he had left it lying at the edge of the camp. He pulled back the zipper to reveal Blain's face, which looked peaceful in death, as if lying in state. The weapon had done no damage here, and the nightfall pale of the last light made the gray of death softer. Gently Mac reached a hand into Blain's shirt pocket and pulled out the flask they had shared earlier in the day.

The worn chrome was rubbed away, revealing the brass beneath. Mac rolled up a shirtsleeve to expose the cleaner face of the rough cotton and carefully rubbed the flask in a circular motion, as if he were polishing a valuable piece of jewelry. The outline of the insignia— 101st airborne division—was still visible on the side. It was the company Mac and Blain had served in together in Nam, fourteen years before.

He removed the cap with a priestly dignity and raised the container to his lips, taking a swig of the sour mash whiskey, careful to leave enough for another hefty shot. Then he replaced the cap, lifted the flap on Blain's shirt pocket and gently pushed the flask back into place.

"I don't know where you're goin', bro," he said, "but two bits says you can use this." Then he lingered a moment and saluted his friend one final time. Then zipped the poncho shut. The dark had fallen completely now.

"Adios, buddy," he whispered.

TWELVE

ONCE THE DUST from the blast had settled and the explosive flashes faded into the murky dusk, the alien shook its head as its vision began to return. It peered down at Hawkins's naked corpse, its prehensile spur piercing deep into the Irishman's thigh as if the body were a side of meat hanging from a butcher's hook. With some difficulty the creature dragged its newest victim through the vine-webbed tangles of jungle like a sack of stones.

It had no concept of the heart loss that attended an earthling death or the rage it had stirred in the surviving commandos. Killing was simply a means to an end and had no more significance than the plowing down of the trees to make room for the spaceship. Only the lower species ever died on the alien's home planet. The higher forms so endlessly transformed themselves that they never inhabited a body long enough to die. They sloughed themselves like snakeskins. Therefore the creature dissected these killer soldiers as dispassionately and as carefully as a clockmaker might dismantle an unusually subtle timepiece.

Obsessively it probed to locate the center of man's

131

identity by analyzing every millimeter of flesh and
bone. Though it hadn't succeeded yet, it had already
figured that the skull and perhaps the spinal cord were
crucial pieces of the puzzle. The rest of the body was
patently clumsy and unimportant—discardable, like
packaging.

The alien hauled the body through the night for about
a half mile till it reached what looked like a dry lake bed
in a thick expanse of cottonwood trees. The lake bed
was like a bowl at the base of a jagged hill five miles
from the Conta Mana border. An odd, surreal bluish
glow filtered through the cottonwood branches, like a
full moon's bathing glow on a clear night, yet here it
shone at ground level like a fallen star, and tinted with
an aqua sheen like the shallows of the Caribbean.

The eerie light emanated from the alien's spacecraft,
which had set down in the middle of the lake bed. Here
was the egg-shaped ship in which the creature had traveled sixteen million miles on its single-minded search
for a sense of self. And for the second time. The lake
bed had been hollowed out by its fiery landing a thousand years before. For this trip it had honed in on automatic pilot.

The oval-shaped craft sat ominously still, its smooth
metallic shell glowing with a copper patina. The alien
stood before it and with a gesture like a blessing raised a
three-fingered hand. A ramp extended from the side of
the ship and lowered to the ground, seemingly suspended on a dozen lasers. The intruder from another
world hefted the bloody body over its shoulder, walked
up into the ship, and slung down its newest prize. The
silence was broken by the dull thump of the body hitting
the cold tungsten floor.

With vastly concentrated strength, its spur still snagged deep in the human flesh, the alien punctured the skin at the base of Hawkins's spine with its other clawlike hand, severing the cord like a knife through butter. Then it bore upward, ripping at the vertebrae. Stubbornly it yanked harder, pulling the entire spine free of the body, a sickly snapping and popping of cartilege echoing off the chamber walls as bone separated from tissue.

Without a trace of emotion the alien bore the head and spine into a further chamber of the ship, leaving a ghostly trail of blood and flesh on the pristine floor. It entered an oval room illumined by an intense blue light. The marauder laid the sacred remains on its autopsy table and stood back, watching as the light from above shifted to a yellowish orange. Then, with the help of laser technology centuries beyond the earth's, the connective tissue clinging to the bones shriveled and disintegrated into tiny mounds of dust.

Then the light changed to a soft green, and the alien lifted the skull column and admired the trophy under the light. It was as smooth and white as a steer's skeleton in the desert picked clean by scavengers and bleached for years by the sun.

The alien reached out and placed it precisely on a glowing shelf along one side of the ship, caressing it gently, proudly, as one might a prized artifact from an ancient civilization. It felt of the texture and stroked the hollows with a haunting detachment. As the green light glowed ever more triumphant it became evident that this was only one of many such trophies displayed around the room. It was some otherworldly equivalent of a big game hunter's headroom, walls covered with elephant tusks and moose antlers. Yet it bore a kind of purity too, like a scientist's lab or the inner sanctum of a temple.

At the makeshift encampment Anna and Billy were staring warily into the trees as the black shade of darkness caused objects to merge in a mass of tricks and shadows. Fueled by their fear, their imaginations played havoc as they gaped at the pitiless jungle, each with his own inadequate god.

Ramirez had just finished setting up Hawkins's radio and began twisting knobs frantically in search of a frequency that would connect the commandos with their lifeline, the standby choppers waiting just over the Conta Mana border. Dillon stood by holding the handset and started to speak as broken crackles of static began to sputter from the speaker.

"Blazer One, Blazer One, come in! Red Fox here. Over."

In return he could hear a barely audible voice garbled with interference. "Blazer One here. Position and status, Red Fox. Over."

Dillon winced nervously. He hadn't ascertained their coordinates but knew they had to be within a few miles of safety—that tantalizing couple of miles that mocked them like a thousand in their sudden danger. "Blazer One, Mayday! We're just over the border near the river. Enemy camp destroyed. Two dead. Guerrillas in pursuit. Need immediate pickup. Circumstances critical. Over."

Interminable seconds passed as the men huddled about the battered radio. Then, through waves of interference, they got their reply. "Request for extraction denied. Your area still compromised. Proceed to Sector three thousand for prisoner extraction, Priority Alpha. Next contact at ten thirty hours."

Dillon's face went pale with rage as he listened to his orders. "Roger, Blazer One. Over and out." He switched off the receiver. "Dumb fuckin' bastards," he growled, turning to the others gathered around. "What the hell do they think this is—tag?"

Schaefer watched Dillon with the hint of a smirk playing about his lips. At last he could hear an echo of the old ghetto fury welling up in his former compatriot.

"What's the matter, Dillon?" teased the major. "Limo outa gas? Expendable assets, pal, *remember?*" He spoke with savage irony. "Seems Langley's never around when you need 'em, huh? We should've requested a little tour in Syria. Transportation's regular, and they got TV cameras up the ass."

"We're still too far in," Dillon replied tightly, ignoring Schaefer's taunts.

But Schaefer wasn't buying Dillon's version anymore. "Bullshit, nigger, you're just like the rest of us now."

The major was thinking to himself that if it weren't for the darker situation of the alien he'd be just as happy to flatten Dillon, whom he thought of now as a coward at worst, at best a hopeless incompetent.

Dillon glared back at Schaefer, silently reading his thoughts, the dead receiver lying useless in his upturned hand. The men waited to see if the confrontation would explode—eager for it, really. But then the major stood up and turned abruptly to Ramirez, who was craning his eyes at the impenetrable canopy of vines and branches.

"Shitload o' good a chopper'd do us in here anyway," the Chicano sneered.

Dillon turned to Mac, determined to establish command again. "Who hit us today?" he asked sharply.

"Don't know, only saw one of 'em," Mac answered vacantly. "Camouflaged, kinda like Spiderman. He was over there . . ." he said, pointing into the rugged chaparral, recalling the chase. His words trailed off with his terrible memories. "Those fucking eyes," he muttered, numb and awestruck. Then he shivered in the steamy night, though the temperature still hovered just under a hundred.

Dillon interrupted impatiently. *"What,* Sergeant?"

"Those eyes!" Mac turned, shaken, glaring at Dillon and shouting angrily. "It was like lookin' straight into hell! But I know one thing," he swore with huge conviction. "I drew down and fired right into its heart. Capped off two hundred rounds and then my pistol— the full pack." His hands were shaking with murderous rage. "Nothin' . . . *nothin'* on this earth coulda' lived, not at that range!" At the end his voice was a roar of defiance, as if he would throttle Dillon if the black man dared to contradict him.

As Dillon digested Mac's fury, the burly soldier stood up and grabbed his gun. "I got the first watch," he declared as he walked away. For all the inexplicable horror he had seen, he was a soldier first. Even in the face of an enemy which seemed unconquerable, the night watch must be kept. Perhaps for Blain's sake as much as anyone's.

As Mac departed Dillon turned to Anna. "What'd *you* see?" he demanded in Spanish. "What happened to the man with the radio?"

The rebel woman replied slowly in broken, halting English. "It was . . . it was the jungle," she stuttered.

The hard edge, the aggressive tension were gone from her now as she retreated passively in fear. She wanted these men's protection, enemy or not. Politics didn't matter anymore. Life did. The American Satan was nothing to the devil she had seen.

"Christ, what the hell . . . ?" Dillon sputtered with exasperation. "Talkin' to you two is like tryin' to sell a freezer to a fuckin' Eskimo! Why can't you give me a straight answer?"

But Anna had closed again like a bruised orchid. Her eyelids drooped, and the old convent prayers came murmuring out of her mouth, lulling her into a peaceful stupor. Dillon wasn't going to get anything more from her. As Ramirez stood nervously by he spotted Billy off to the side of the group by himself. The Sioux was meditating on the night-curtained jungle around him—aware, catlike, absorbing every sound, his nerves live like cinders in a fire. Ramirez approached the wiry Indian. "You know somethin', don't you, Billy boy?" he asked. "What is it? Tell your pointman."

Billy turned to look at Ramirez, his face frozen, eyes black and wide as the onyx orbs of a Mayan idol. "I'm scared," he said, and the simple hush of the remark was more horrible than a blood-curdling scream.

To Ramirez's knowledge Billy Sole had never been scared in his life—or at least he'd never admitted it. For this stoic soldier to yield to fear made Ramirez suddenly feel like he was standing naked and weaponless in a lion's den. The spunky barrio tough was chilled to the marrow. Almost in desperation Ramirez tried to coax the Indian out of his terror as if it would still his own. "Bullshit, man! You ain't afraid of nothin'!" It sounded strangely like a threat.

Billy stood firm, his feet spread in an animal crouch. He looked Ramirez straight in the eyes. Although Billy had seen no more of the actual creature than anyone else—less, in fact, than Mac and Anna—he'd looked deeper than all the rest in his trance.

"There's something waiting for us out there," he whispered, inches from Ramirez's face. "And it's not guerrillas, my friend. It's not about war, and it's not about weapons, and nobody's gonna win."

Dillon, who'd caught fragments of the interaction, thought Billy must be spooked. "He's just losin' his cool," Dillon explained archly to the speechless Ramirez as the Indian wandered off. "There's nothing out there but a couple of shitass pinko guerrillas we're gonna take down," he insisted stubbornly, as sure of their superior power as his CIA brethren had been during the bombing of North Vietnam. But despite the force of his words there was a razor's edge of doubt in his voice, and both men knew it.

Schaefer strode back over as the conversation petered out, leaving Dillon alone with no one to order around. The major was holding his hand up, gripping the clutch of dogtags taken from Davis's slaughtered men. He shoved them in Dillon's face.

"Still don't get it, do you, Dillon?" he growled, his voice a mix of grief and fury and helplessness. "He took Davis, and now he wants us."

The jungle lay in a hot, inert, and inky darkness, though a crisp three-quarter moon drifted in and out of the canyon mist, now and then breaking clear and shedding a cool glow over the trees. Mac was hunched in his foxhole staring into the night, his weapon set on a tripod before him. His eyes kept catching phantoms as he gazed at the dense forest. Leaves became hands, vines snakes. The brutal events of the day were sufficient to unbalance even this most battle-scarred vet's hard-edged attitude. He kept thinking of another time years ago south of Khe San when he and Blain had survived another nightmare trap. He began to whisper aloud to himself as if he were back in the mud and smoke, crawling overland to Penong Bay, Blain at his side.

"Same kinda jungle," he murmured. "Same winkin' moon and everything, bro'. A real number ten night, remember? Just you and me, mud up our fuckin' noses, the only guys in the whole platoon who made it out in one piece."

As his eyes darted about anxiously, he recalled that earlier night so vividly he could no longer distinguish it from now. "We crawled out right under their noses, didn't we?" he continued with a dry laugh. "Not a scratch. No fuckin' chili-choker'd ever get to you, bro'," he drawled with pride. "You was just too good. Hell, if you don't stay in one piece, then neither do I. That's a deal, okay?"

Then Mac shook himself back to the present, and a rush of anger took over.

"I promise you this, bro'," he swore with murderous intensity, the blood oath ringing in the jungle dark. "Whoever he is, I hope he's plannin' to hit us again . . . 'cause he's got my name on him, like a fuckin' tattoo on his forehead!"

An electron force field surrounded the alien's ship as the creature, now on the prowl again full-scale, came gliding down the laser-suspended ramp and out into the humid night. As it stepped from the beam of light to the rugged ground its humanoid form merged with the night's moonless shadows. But its masquerade went much further than the coincidence of shadow play. For the remarkable being had set another of its defensive techniques into motion. Now its very cells began to swirl and integrate with the night air until there was no sign of the creature at all.

It was as if it had realized from observing the commandos the importance of absolute camouflage, especially under cover of darkness.

Thus, unlike the earlier incident of the cloning of the hawk, this time it didn't require a host animal to receive. It simply vanished, its whole substance, tissue, skin, organs, coasting on the jungle breezes, dispersed and invisible. The tracks in the soft dirt stopped a few yards from the ship at the edge of the clearing, so that a tracker like Billy might have supposed the creature had flown off into the sky. But no—it was as disparate now as a virus. And it was on the hunt again, foraging toward the remaining commandos.

Now that it had satisfied itself with a thorough examination of Hawkins's body it was impatient for a new specimen, perhaps something even more advanced.

As the alien disappeared into the darkness, the lasers silently retracted and the ramp withdrew, becoming flush with the spacecraft's glimmering surface, not a hint of a seam joint. The craft became an impenetrable shell, pure and pregnant as an egg. Then its glossy copper-colored exterior began to fade and cloud. It too was becoming one with the night, just as its captain had moments before. Soon it held its place invisible as a god.

THIRTEEN

AT THE COMMANDO camp the mountain mist had thickened, and the canyon night was alive with the crackle and hoot and screech of the prowler beasts. A few of the team managed to nod off for a few restless moments at a time, but the men were so wired and on edge that true rest was mostly impossible. The spent commandos were operating on sheer raw nerve—headachy, cranky, and exhausted, yet forced to a state of alertness by the consuming fear of an enemy they still couldn't name.

Ramirez squatted a few feet from Mac and turned to the brawny vet. "You got any more smoke, buddy?"

"Shit, no. Toked the last one while the boss was givin' that spick whore the third degree. No offense, ya' lousy wetback." Mac coughed and chuckled comfortably at his own good-natured racial slurs.

"Eat shit and die, asshole," Ramirez shot back. Then he laughed heartily too, and they winked at each other.

Yet even as they played this game Mac noticed a sudden change in the background noise. He crossed his lips with a forefinger to silence Ramirez because he'd noticed an odd lull in one quadrant of the jungle darkness. The normal scurrying rodents frantic for a safe harbor from hungry predators, the calls of baboons teasing and warning each other of a stalking cheetah—all had turned dead quiet in the north/northeast. Mac instantly gripped the trigger of his gun barrel, his jaw clenched.

Then somewhere off in the trees a barely negligible metallic click signaled the sound of a warning flare rocketing over the area. A moment later a brilliant flash exploded as the flare burst into flame, momentarily illuminating the camp as if a shooting star had hurtled by.

Then an echoing scream filled the night as a startled intruder ran roughshod through the undergrowth toward the men, branches cracking, the dull thump of heavy feet growing louder. Yet the commotion was so fast, and the misty shadows and canyon night so full of richocheted sound, no one could tell what was charging into the camp.

But the attacking creature was making a beeline straight toward Mac, who stood aiming his M-202 at the unidentified enemy. It broke through a last gnarled bramble and leaped with a roar for the throat of the tough soldier, knocking him into his foxhole.

Mac hollered in stunned surprise, and the rest of the men rushed to the side of the darkened pit, where it was impossible to distinguish Mac from the enemy he battled. Grunts and inhuman growling rose from the foxhole as the commandos stood by helplessly, reluctant to fire for fear of injuring Mac. It was as if each man were standing defenseless at his own grave.

A few final bursts from the flare briefly illuminated the foxhole, yet still they could not separate the two clenched and thrashing figures. Then for a second a blinding gleam startled the men in the circle as Mac's machete caught the light like an ancient warrior's sword.

The sky faded to dark again as the flare burned itself out. Just then a geyser of blood shot up from the hole, splattering on Schaefer's boot. Following that a high-pitched scream—unmistakably a death cry—reverberated off the canyon walls. But whose? Tortured seconds passed as the men waited anxiously for the dust to settle, for the victor—if there was one—to stand. All guns were aimed at the pit in case Mac had been the loser.

Silence had replaced the sounds of struggle. Then a figure slowly pulled himself up, grunting a sigh and propping himself against the crumbling wall of the fox-hole. It was Mac, covered in sweat and dirt, gasping for breath, clothes shredded and bloodied, his knife dangling limply at his side. He looked up directly at Schaefer, his chest heaving as he gulped in the humid night air and whispered hoarsely. "Got the mother-fucker," he grinned between gasps.

The major snapped on a flashlight and raked the fox-hole. Lying in a pool of blood—Mac's and its own—stretched a massive wild boar still quivering in the final throes of death.

For the first time Mac had a clear look at his opponent and stared in disbelief at the creature that almost killed him.

"A pig . . ." he muttered with an edge of disappointment, shame almost. ". . . just a fuckin' pig?"

Schaefer slowly shined his light the full length of the animal. Its deadly sharp tusks gleamed like a weird trophy in the light. Ramirez peered over the edge and looked down in awe.

"Holy shit, Mac!" the Chicano exclaimed. "Shove an apple in the fucker's mouth, and that oughta feed us for a month!"

Mac snarled up at the Mexican in mock anger. "I ain't plannin' on stayin' around here long enough for dinner. She's all yours, buddy."

With the men's attention focused on the dead animal Anna took advantage of the moment's distraction. A confused recollection of her cause returned to mind, and she hustled to make a quick escape. She stooped and picked up an MP-5 from the ground with her bound hands. Then she turned, staring into the mist-enshrouded night for a way out.

But even as she moved forward a few yards her fears of what might be waiting in the dark came rushing back, clouding her sense of resolution again. She stopped and looked up at the opaque sky, and the dim round of the moon played above the trees like a magic eye. For a second she imagined she could feel the gaze of the alien's golden honeycomb eyes piercing the mist. She remembered the spearing of Hawkins with a moan of horror. She abandoned the idea of running and dropped the gun to the ground.

By now the major and Ramirez had dragged the still shaking Mac from the foxhole. A huge gash ripped across the thatch of hair on the victor's chest, one of the boar's brute attempts to skewer him on its deadly tusks.

"Get a field dressing on him right away," Schaefer instructed harshly. This whole scene seemed all wrong. The violence was crude and stupid, and the enemy was dumb. It was almost like a mockery of the real horror that lay in wait in the jungle fog.

Ramirez ran to grab the medic's bag as Billy, who'd

been scouting the perimeter beyond the foxholes, called out. "Major, over here!" he shouted urgently.

Schaefer turned apprehensively, something dire in Billy's tone warning him that the Indian had discovered something bad and irreversible. Dutch walked with bitter resignation toward the scout, whom he found standing with a flashlight pointed at the canvas bag that had cradled Blain's body. It was violently slashed open, covered in blood, empty.

The Sioux looked up at the major and spoke the obvious, as if he found some weird comfort in sticking strictly to the facts. "The body's gone," he said flatly.

Ramirez came running up. He had patched Mac up, then made a quick tour and checked out the trip wires surrounding the camp. "Came in through the wires," he reported. "Took him right out from under our noses."

Anna, once more seeking the security of the men, appeared at their side and stared down into the empty, blood-soaked bag. Then she glanced anxiously into Schaefer's eyes. The major knew from her stricken look that she sensed, she knew the horror that had driven her mind astray was not just a nightmare. The body bag woke her up for good. She looked as if she would never sleep again.

Hours passed in a grim silence, each of the men turned in on himself and hunkered above his weapon. Slowly the blue-black predawn sky offered a hushed clarity, and the men's imaginations were calmed by the gathering light. A patchy ground fog still covered the area. Anna, who'd finally been overtaken by sleep, awoke with a start in her foxhole, the rising cacaphony of early morning jungle music reaching its high-pitched tempo. A blue-tail monkey screamed at a cropping mountain goat. A cheetah yawned and turned belly up, fat and sleepy from a night of eating a side of deer.

Directly above Anna's head a chameleon emerged on a leaf. Carefully the rebel woman extended her arm, allowing the lizard to crawl onto her, watching fascinated as it changed color to match her tawny skin tone. Then she gently placed the creature back on the leaf and watched with a half-smile as it changed once more to a cool green and glided into the jungle.

Schaefer, Billy, and Ramirez were busy examining the area near the empty bag, poring over every inch of trip wire, worrying the ground for signs and hints of what happened.

"Boar set off the trip," Billy reported to Schaefer finally. "No other tracks."

Schaefer knelt and examined the thin, well-hidden stretch of wire, with the ash-gray short in the copper where the boar's hoof had connected. Then the major stood, looking around the makeshift camp. The canyon below was slowly steaming clear of mist.

"How the hell could anything get through this setup and carry Blain out?" observed Ramirez with brooding frustration. "And they did it right under the light of a flare without leaving a fuckin' trace." The Chicano kicked a rock in frustration, exploding a nest of centipedes that scurried away in panic.

Schaefer considered the possibilities, his eyes drawing a bead on the tree line as if it were a graph. "He's using the trees," he said at last, pointing to the thick-crowned cottonwoods. "The bastard knows our defenses," he went on bitterly.

Then he caught his own use of the singular noun. Instinctively he'd concluded this was not the work of a team. There was nothing guerrillalike about it. It was the macabre work of a singular enemy, and thus the logic sided more and more with Billy's story.

In his mind Schaefer traced the path the intruder might have traveled through the trees, then down to the ground where it could've hopped the trip wire. But what sort of creature could move like that he didn't have a clue. What he did know was that they were dealing with a remarkable villain, cunning beyond anything Schaefer had witnessed in Thailand, Beirut, or any other blood-hole of the world.

Somehow, it seemed, this enemy flew through the trees with the dexterity of a monkey and across open turf with the speed and agility of a jaguar. On top of that it possessed the strength of ten gorillas and the subtle stealth of all the wildcats of the jungle combined. God knew what else it could do. And so far there'd been no sign of even a knife or a pistol, let alone the kind of high-tech combat gear the commandos carried. So far, Schaefer thought grimly, there wasn't a sign of anything human.

As the major squinted along the dawn-streaked treeline, Billy and Ramirez stood rigid and motionless, glaring blankly in among the branches, seeming to share a dread as acute as their mutual feel for the flow of a trail. It was becoming clear to each of the remaining commandos that they were up against terrible odds. Ramirez, normally the tough, abrasive street kid, blunt and not given to asking questions, suddenly revealed a rare twinge of anxiety. "Why didn't he try to kill one of us last night?" he asked in the meek tones of a child afraid to sleep without a night light.

Schaefer turned abruptly to him. "He came back for

the body," he replied coldly. "He's killing us one at a time. . . ."

"Predator," Billy stated flatly, his face showing no emotion.

Schaefer was sick and tired of vague explanations. He turned to Anna, their only concrete witness. He reached down, his eyes blazing and his jaw tensed, and yanked her firmly to her feet.

"Yesterday, what'd you see?"

She stared back at the major vacantly. But Schaefer's insisting expression seemed to shake her out of her trance. She struggled to keep reality clear. The major was determined to drag the information out of her if he had to cut out her tongue, but he saw at least she was struggling to respond. She began to speak slowly.

"I . . . don't know . . . what it was," she started, then balked as a rush of tears filled her eyes. She had a terrible longing to confess to the old drunken priest at the convent school.

"Go on," Schaefer persisted, more gently now.

"It changes color," she continued haltingly. "Just like the chameleon. It uses the jungle and hides . . ."

Dillon cut her off, his ear for the truth limited to what he could see, feel, and measure. "Shit, lady, you tryin' to tell me those guys were killed by a fuckin' *lizard?* Don't listen to her, man," he raged at Schaefer. "It's just a guerrilla con job—a sure as shit con job! She's tryin' to get our defenses down!"

Schaefer ignored the black man's ranting and cut the hard-line approach to the frightened girl. He reached out and took her hands and looked directly at her starshot eyes.

"What's your name?" he asked quietly.

She gazed back into his own calm unblinking eyes, momentarily cautious as to this sudden new tactic. She hesitated a second, then gave in, so needful was she for a little tenderness. "Anna," she whispered. "Anna Gonsalves." She sounded as modest as if she were talking to the mother superior.

"Listen to me, Anna Gonsalves," Schaefer replied in a parental tone, stern but reassuring. "You know we have the same enemy now, don't you?"

She nodded in grave agreement.

Still looking her squarely in the eyes the major drew out his commando knife and carefully sliced through her rope bonds with a single sweep of the blade.

Dillon was stunned. "Fuck, Dutch, what the hell you think you're doin'?" he bawled, eyes wide with outrage.

Not taking his eyes off the dark-haired girl, the major acknowledged Dillon wearily, with no small hint of condescension. "No more prisoners, Dillon. We need everybody now."

"What are you talkin' about?"

"We're not goin' anywhere, Dillon," Schaefer said briskly, his tone more along the lines of an order than a suggestion.

"You outa your mind?" The black leader slapped at an elephant leaf in frustration. He could see that Schaefer was serious but had no idea what the strategy was. "We're only two, maybe three miles from the border, tops," he went on helplessly. "We're almost home, Dutch. That chopper's not gonna wait. We gotta go!"

Schaefer turned away from Anna and faced the black man head on. He spoke with brute authority. "Face it, Dillon. You know as well as I do we're just part of somebody's game. And he don't give a fuck who we are or who she is. This has nothin' to do with your shit-ass little war game. You want another stripe on that pretty starched uniform, hotshot? Well, we don't take a stand now you're not even goin' to make it over the next anthill alive. You can forget Langley and all your ass-kissin' cousins, pardner. None of it's gonna do you a shitload of good lyin' here with your guts carved out!"

Dillon blinked back, knowing full well that Schaefer was on-target. He didn't want to hear what he already knew to be true, but he couldn't hide from it anymore, either. Not all the statistics and paperwork in the world could mask the horror that hovered palpably all around them now.

Anna, sensing a lull in the heated exchange between the two soldiers, reached out and touched Schaefer's arm. Somehow she understood he was to be trusted now, and she was determined to help all the way. She was drawn to Schaefer's strength, startled at the magnitude of his physical power. None of her comrades exuded this kind of command. "There's something else," she said urgently. "When the big man was killed, one of you must have wounded the thing. Its blood rubbed off on the leaves." And she reached down and pointed to the fading amber stain on her pants leg.

Schaefer turned to Dillon with a tight grin. "If it bleeds we can kill it," he announced matter-of-factly. "All we need's a shot at it. So let's get loaded up, huh? I want to nail me a Martian."

FOURTEEN

NOW THAT ANNA had become an unofficial team member, her role changed radically. She sat crouched at the base of the rocks just beyond the encampment, scanning the tree line with binoculars. Mac maneuvered by her, uncoiling a new trip wire linking four claymore mines camouflaged by leaves and branches at strategic points around the camp. In a tree at the edge of the clearing Billy tossed a roll of wire to Ramirez, who wound it around a grenade wedged in the crotch of a cottonwood's branches. When they'd finished, every inch of ground surrounding the camp to a radius of thirty meters was booby-trapped, all except for a single narrow corridor for getting out and down the canyon trail.

At the end of the path where the rock outcropping merged with the jungle Schaefer hauled down a heavy vine about four inches in diameter, straining with every ounce of strength, biceps bulging and glistening with sweat. On the other side of the path Dillon took up the slack of the vine around the base of a rubber tree. Like a fisherman at his nets the major took the free end of the vine and attached it to a forty-foot sapling, arcing the sapling closer to the ground with every pull, till it formed a gigantic bow creaking and groaning with tension. With a final mighty heave the major drew the sapling enough within reach to grip the top branches, then gestured to Dillon to tie it off.

Dillon assisted with some reluctance. He knew if he didn't cooperate he'd be about as welcome here as at a KKK meeting. But the part of him that needed to be in charge couldn't refrain from ragging Schaefer, whom he saw as usurping his authority steadily, inch by inch. Effectively this was so, but Schaefer didn't see it that way. He was just trying to get a job done, and though the job required a commando's skills, it had nothing to do with soldiering anymore and so was beyond the need of a chain of command. In some way now it was every man for himself.

"I'm tellin' you, we're wasting what little time we got left," Dillon argued truculently. "This snare shit isn't gonna stop guerrillas. All we're doing is letting the rest of 'em catch up with us."

Schaefer had long ago learned when to turn off his attention and thus ignored Dillon entirely. The major continued to secure the vine, then dragged a net into position, crudely woven of rubber branches, leaves still attached. Methodically he began to cover the net with more leaves and debris. Just maybe they could catch a monster in the same ancient way the Mayans caught their sacred jaguars.

Dutch moved swiftly, picking up a framework of whittled sticks he had tied together as a crude spring trigger. He held up the makeshift contraption, hurriedly examining his work for flaws before fixing it in place at the edge of the net.

"He'll be looking for trip wires. If we're lucky he won't see this," he explained absently to Dillon.

"What's this 'he' shit?" countered the black man. "You sound like we're waitin' for one guy. There's an *army* out there, Major!"

"Can it, Dillon! The bastard who's after us now's no pinko contra. It ain't that simple anymore. Look, I'm heading back to the others. You coming, or you wanna stay here like a sitting duck?"

Dillon followed sullenly as the major walked away. But he couldn't bear not to get in a last dig. "Now what, Dutch? You gonna send your mystery guest an invitation?"

Schaefer stopped and swiveled around, staring at the black man. "Now you're catchin' on, smartass. Maybe we're gonna save your little dick after all." Schaefer laughed gruffly and turned away again, completely discarding any further notion of rank and protocol. To him Dillon was just another pain in the butt now.

The sticky morning passed excruciatingly slow, and a humid tropical fog loomed as heavy as the tedious minutes. By noon the sun had crept through, white and exhausted, and the visibility gradually returned. A half hour later the pulsing rays glistened on the beads of sweat that coated every leaf, every mossy surface. The jungle danced as usual—swarms of bees in the orchids, swoops of hungry birds, hyenas lurking patiently in the shadows waiting for a gorged jaguar to leave a tapir lunch behind.

The commandos sat stoically silent, heavily camouflaged with leaves twisted about their caps, huddled in the twisted brambles of their camp. They waited motionless as statues, fixated on the twisted vegetation growing rampant on the canyon rim around them. They'd done all they could to prepare for the alien's next attack, using every glimmer of initiative they could think of for defense, turning to the jungle itself for help —as with the vine snare braced to snap if an intruder so much as breathed on its trigger. But so far the only sounds were the normal lulling hum and buzz of the jungle, seemingly unchanged for a thousand years.

Then all at once, between one minute and the next, a veil of silence descended over the jagged highlands of the interior. The major couldn't tolerate the waiting any longer, and he stirred like a cougar cornered in its lair. He nodded to Ramirez, indicating that he was moving out to check the trap. Slowly he stood, his senses burning, the silence growing louder in his head like an inner scream. He walked carefully along the narrow leaf-shrouded corridor while the others sighted down their hidden gun barrels, covering Schaefer from three angles, all the while scanning the canyon for the slightest hint of sound or movement.

As the major reached the primitive trap, meticulously skirting the various triggers that could snap him off his feet in a flash, he stopped and waited, sweat pouring down his face and neck, drenching his already clinging shirt. A green snake slithered near his feet, and he flinched slightly but couldn't afford to lose his focus on the vastness around him. Something was nearby, hiding and waiting. He could practically feel it breathe. His fingers tightened on the trigger of his M-202.

Quickly he spun around to glance behind. Then he came around again full circle and waved his gun from left to right. Nothing. Not a hint, yet the continuing silence tipped him off that something dangerous was out there. Finally he turned back to the camp, his taut face registering a kind of disappointment that he hadn't encountered the enemy. A face-to-face would surely be better than all this elusiveness.

He marched briskly toward the others, feeling hollow and defeated. It was Billy he went to first, hoping now for even some sign from the magic world he so resisted. But as he approached, the Indian shook his head in grim bewilderment. Dillon rose and strode over to the two of them. He had an 'I told you so' smirk written across his face. "Satisfied?" he demanded sarcastically. "Now can we get the hell out of here?"

Just then, from the end of the corridor by the snare, a loud swish followed by the snapping of branches broke the silence. An instant later the net exploded off the jungle floor in a hail of leaves and sticks, rocketing up into a stand of mahogany trees growing tightly together. Schaefer jerked his head around, and the whole team leaped to its feet as the trap went off. Even at this distance they could see that a huge struggling creature mauled the sides of the net, and a long unearthly high-pitched screech echoed through the canyon.

Schaefer led the commandos down the short incline along the corridor toward the bobbing net. All their guns were cocked. Only Anna remained behind, crouching behind a rocky outcropping, terrified and praying.

As they arrived under the net it was beginning to tear beneath the strain of its victim's powerful thrusts. Then the whole network of branches exploded into smithereens of vine and leaves and dirt. A streak of pulsating crimson leaped for the trees, and a powerful three-fingered hand gripped at a limb. It was the alien, at the height of day, raging scarlet and mercurial beneath the brilliant sun without any camouflage at all.

As the men watched, appalled and mesmerized, the creature shook off the last traces of vegetation. With its free arm it pulled its weapon out of nowhere, the sharp spearhead gleaming in the sunlight. Its mouth roared with fury, and with one sweep it slashed angrily at a limb eight inches thick, severing the heavy wood and sending it plummeting to the ground.

Ramirez didn't see the severed limb in time, and it struck him with a thudding blow to the shoulder, lifting him off his feet and hurling him backward into the underbrush. When he landed his shirt was torn from belly to shoulder, exposing a deep gouge in his chest that erupted with spurts of black-red blood.

Then with an easy leap the alien dropped to a lower branch fifteen feet from the ground, just above the soldiers' heads. They watched in frozen horror. Meanwhile, some kind of instinct took over Anna as soon as she saw Ramirez fall, and she ran down the hill to his aid. The alien's physical presence had shocked her back to reality, and the reality she was struck by told her the commandos were her only hope. The more of the team that remained alive, the better all their odds would be.

The stunned commandos gaped at the creature, momentarily paralyzed as they confronted it for the first time, naked and in its humanoid form, close enough to touch. Its lizard skin was pulsating deep vermilion now, in high contrast to the lush green of the surroundings. It clung to the side of the tree like a terrible hellish gargoyle, snarling and hissing like a siren, full of enormous hate.

Dillon, more dumbfounded than the rest because

he'd been so stubbornly resistant to the signs, was the first to speak. "What in God's name . . ." he whispered.

As the black man spoke, the alien let loose with a loud penetrating trill, its wide red mouth agape, revealing sawtooth fangs. A moment later its color modulated and swirled with blues and greens until the creature seemed to bleed into the leaves, invisible again. Mac opened fire on the disappearing form, shredding the limb and leaves it clutched. But it was already too late. The alien was gone. Fevered and wild, Mac raved madly into the jungle after it.

Schaefer bellowed. "Mac! Mac, come back! You don't know where the hell it went!" The major snapped the empty clip from his rifle and inserted a new one while barking an order to Billy. "Get Ramirez and the girl, and get out of here! Now!"

Then he started off through the trees after Mac. But immediately Dillon stepped in his path, a hand pushing against Schaefer's chest. "No way, Dutch. *I'm* going. You take the rest and get the hell over the border."

"This is no time to play hero, Dillon," Schaefer retorted, surprised at the black man's toughness.

"Guess I've picked up some bad habits from you, Dutch," Dillon replied. "Now don't argue with me. Not only am I your commanding officer, but you also know I'm right. Get to that chopper and hold it for us. I'll find Mac and we'll be right behind you."

"Dillon, you can't win this one." The major was almost touched by Dillon's sincerity. There was a glimmer here of the man he would have laid down his life for once.

The black soldier stared back defiantly. He was beginning to show the stripes he wore. "You know me,

Dutch. I never did know when to quit. How'm I ever gonna be the first black president if I don't learn how to walk through the fire?"

For the first time on this mission Schaefer felt a rush of feeling for the old Dillon. The major backed down now with more than a touch of respect for the man. It was a strange experience for a loner like Schaefer to find himself proud to obey the man who was supposed to be in charge all along.

As Dillon moved out Schaefer called after him. "Hey, buddy! Take this!" As the top man turned back, Schaefer tossed him a spare MP-5. Dillon snatched it out of the air with one hand. They shared an utterly naked look, a look that said their differences were settled. It was also a look of farewell—these were men who kept their bases covered. "I'll see you at the chopper," Schaefer said with a dreadful hollow certainty that he would never see the man alive again.

"Right behind you," Dillon called back. The black man had truly left his desk behind as he hefted both weapons at the hip and trotted off into the jungle after Mac. Schaefer watched him go for a moment, then turned back to Ramirez, who was now sitting up with Anna's and Billy's help. He was holding his ribs and gasping for breath.

"He's busted up pretty bad, Major," Billy reported.

"Fuck you, Tonto," the wiry Chicano snarled while wheezing for air. "I can make it. Help me up." And he held a hand out to his brother scout. Schaefer walked over and gripped an arm around Ramirez for support. "Come on, Poncho," he said, "we're gettin' outa here. Billy, take the radio and leave the rest of this stuff. Let's move!"

As the foursome limped along the canyon rim, looking for a downhill trail that would feed them out over
the border, Mac was a quarter mile away, creeping low
to the ground, his eyes searching the trees. "C'mon, you
motherfucker," he whispered urgently.

About three hundred yards behind Mac, Dillon was
tracking through the underbrush, straining to zero in on
a faint rustling in the foliage up ahead. Was it Mac? At
first the sound was too vague and sporadic to identify.
The black man froze, listening harder, and began to
make out a barely audible voice. "Dillon, over here,"
the words came whispering through the trees.

Cautiously the commander of the mission moved
ever closer to the sound, parting the leaves like curtains,
then heard the voice again. "Dillon . . . psst . . . over
here." And the black man ducked through a tangle of
vines and entered a small dark clearing, almost claustro-
phobic with the density of the highland foliage on every
side, gripping the jagged canyon stone. Dillon looked
around a full 360 degrees but saw nothing except the
endless wall of jungle.

"Mac?" Dillon whispered in no particular direction.
Just as he spoke, a hand darted out of the brush and
covered the commander's mouth. He choked with terror
as Mac pulled him into his hiding place in a rift between
chunks of canyon granite.

"It's out there," Mac pointed breathlessly. "Behind
that rock. Can you see it?"

Dillon strained his eyes as if to will them to see
clearer and deeper. After a long moment he thought he
saw a slight movement where Mac had gestured.

"I think I got a glimpse," Dillon whispered back.
"Let's take him out, huh?" he added impatiently. Then

he hastily outlined a simple attack plan to his fellow commando, who for the first time found himself in agreement with this slick-edged soldier he thought had gone soft. Dillon jabbed a finger toward a rock outcropping strangled by masses of creeper vines about a hundred feet away. "Take a cover position over there. I'll work around toward you. When I flush him out you nail him."

"Gotcha," Mac agreed without an instant's hesitation. "Listen, I got a score to settle for the Bro'."

"We *both* got scores to settle," Dillon corrected him. It was as if Dillon had done some hard reflecting on his own role in this mission so far, and he wasn't pleased at all with the deceit. True, it had been thought necessary for the highest national security purposes, but finally so what? It had also been the source of the tension between Schaefer, the team, and himself. Somehow he wanted to make up for all the crossed feelings, and he knew that wiping out the mutant creature was the one way to do it.

Silently Dillon disappeared into the jungle. Mac watched him vanish among the vine-locked boulders, then made his own way toward the target, working round the razor-sharp rocks and heaving himself through the masses of vines. It was a brief distance, but a rugged journey, trying to move quietly and invisibly through the knotted confusion of the high jungle. The place seemed more primeval, less touched by man, than any ground they'd tröd so far. It was the site of some vast Darwinian nakedness, prehuman and without remorse. Mac cursed himself as a branch snapped back in his face or a vine grasped at his leg. But finally he made it to the rocky spur, settled into position, and scanned the jungle below. He could see Dillon moving off to his left several meters away, his face intense and determined.

Vague, unidentifiable sounds echoed through the clotted canyon forest as Mac pulled himself forward. Then he caught a fleeting image of movement in the foliage ahead. He began to sweat bullets as recollections of the hideous blood-red creature crowded into his mind. Was it out there waiting? He recalled the row of dead men hanging gutted, their insides spilled and their faces twisted in anguish. He forced the thought from his mind, switched the safety catch off his rifle, and reached up for another vine to pull himself even higher.

He felt a queer warm movement beneath his grip. He didn't even have time to react as the vine began to crawl around his fingers. A second later he was horrified to see the sinewy green bark change even as he gripped it, till he was suddenly holding the clawlike hand of the alien. It ripped loose from Mac's grip, flipped around in a swirl of flashing prehensile fingers, and grabbed the commando by the wrist.

The stunned soldier looked up in time to see the creature's two burning yellow eyes piercing down at him like burning liquid starlight, just as its other hand swooped to his throat, its razor-sharp spur slashing through his windpipe. Mac pitched forward, instantly dead, and landed with a thud in a scatter of moldering leaves. His heart, still pumping, gushed out spurts of blood from his severed jugular. It was all done quietly, smoothly, quickly, and life ran away in a meaningless ooze, to be swallowed up by the famished jungle floor.

FIFTEEN

NEARBY DILLON HEARD a faint disturbance, then silence. He shrugged and moved on, stalking down a narrow alley between two clusters of vines leading to the
sheer rock wall. His face was utterly alert, showing no
signs of fear, his weapon ready. He sensed a slight
movement ahead, an undulating distortion that drifted
through the hanging vegetation as if an errant breeze
had passed.

The black man stopped, ears and eyes burning. The
hints of movement were so slight he couldn't be certain
if his imagination were playing tricks with the steaming
jungle.

It was the alien, of course, drawing out the game of
stalking just like cat-and-mouse. It had won so many
battles now that it seemed to take the time to savor the
thrill of the chase, as if testing its own skill and mastery
over this elusive creature man. But also like the cat it
only appeared to be playing. In its mind, its emotionless
brain, it was simply honing its wits and combat tactics,
as if it would move from this border war to clash with
whole worlds. It synchronized its own movements to
match Dillon's precisely, and its sounds and silences

were timed to the pulsebeat with the black man's. So that when Dillon stopped to listen, the alien froze at exactly the same instant.

Still, the soldier sensed its presence. Dillon crouched and spun around, leveling his rifle at the black-green background. Yet the path he had taken was undisturbed, silent. Nothing in the lie of the trail suggested the presence of a predator. But as he scanned the brace of rubber trees behind him he didn't realize that for an instant he looked directly into the alien's eyes. The creature was peering out from the crook of a tree, examining his prey. But the golden eyes were so otherworldly that Dillon didn't even register them as he searched the jungle. He saw them yet he didn't. They were like a pair of yellow hummingbirds or a couple of orchids or a nest of fireflies, just more of the same tropical excess. So the black man turned and moved on, and the alien resumed its prowl, continuing to match the man's movements, footfall by footfall.

Dillon made it to the granite outcrop expecting to find Mac in place. He signaled with a whistle very like Schaefer's. No response. Then he turned cautiously from left to right. "Mac . . . Mac," he whispered eagerly, beginning to get a bit anxious about being alone.

As he moved closer to the rock wall he literally stumbled over Mac's face, which was staring up at him with a ghastly pallor, eyes frozen wide in death. Dillon cringed, then spun around as if expecting the alien to be right behind him. But again he was faced with the blank solid wall of undergrowth and no sign of the attacker. He looked from one side of the path to the other. Then something iridescent among the vines caught his attention, and he stared hard at a fall of tree moss.

For a moment the afternoon sun and forest shadows blended at the perfect angle for Dillon to catch a flash of the alien's yellow eyes. As quickly as they materialized they disappeared, but at last there was no mistaking them for any other aberrant bit of lushness. Dillon pulled up his rifle, sighted it swiftly and let go a rapid round into the tangle of moss where the eyes had teased him. The vegetation exploded into fragments, but already it was too late.

The alien had leaped aside, and as the dust and leaves were flying in a hundred directions it activated its weapon, seeming to erupt it from its arm, then hurling the spear at Dillon. It slashed easily through the black man's upper arm, severing it above the elbow. The bloody appendage, its nerves tingling as if it were still attached to his body, landed on the ground ten feet away. It flinched and jerked, and the hand still gripping the trigger fired a last round of bullets into the sky.

Dillon screamed in agony as blood gushed from the stump left dangling from his shoulder. Yet with his good arm he still managed to fire the second gun, shouting crazily as he swung it in the direction of the creature. Yet his vision was blurred by the pain, and like Hawkins before him he hit nothing but trees. Even as he fired uselessly the alien recoiled its weapon and hurled it at Dillon's abdomen, which burst open as if sliced by a samurai sword. Eyes popping, with one last gasp of frustrated rage, Dillon lurched over dead. His smooth manicured bureaucrat's finger uncurled from the trigger, and no one at Langley would ever know that their desk man had died in heroic combat.

As Dillon was being slaughtered Anna led the three commandos along the rocky slope leading down the

canyon from the camp to the river. Schaefer followed
behind with Ramirez hoisted on his back while Billy
covered the three of them as he walked slightly above
on the ridge, the radio strapped to his back. Other than a
rifle for each man and a few piddling rounds of ammunition they were down to machetes and a couple of grenades. They knew it would never be enough firepower
for a confrontation.

The water was deep and treacherous, so they dragged
a log to the river's edge to try to make a partial bridge
for getting across. But they froze as they heard the burst
of Dillon's gunfire. They all looked at one another like
grave and desolate children playing a macabre game of
musical chairs.

"C'mon," Schaefer decided quickly. "Let's at least
get Ramirez across before anything else happens."

The alien was racing through the jungle at full speed
now, leaping, tearing, flying from tree to tree in a mad
triumph and leaving a wake of churning jungle heat as if
a meteor were soaring by. It arrived at the river just as
the four survivors were about to shove off. Billy was
closest to the shore at the foot of the log, providing
cover. As the alien drew closer the Indian knew the
enemy had arrived, though he couldn't see it yet, and he
stood and turned to face his ancient destiny.

Stripping down to his raw warrior heritage, he
shrugged the radio off his back and let it slip to the
rocky riverbed. Several dials smashed on the stones, but
the Indian didn't notice. They were beyond radio help
now. Billy was totally focused on his encounter with the
creature. It was as if he understood he had a score to
settle for all the hundreds of ancestors the alien had
slaughtered long ago. A Sioux defending his ancestors

died the noblest death of all.

Billy cast away his rifle and stared intently into the trees. He reached into his cargo pocket and withdrew a small grease-paint tin. Without looking down he dipped his finger into the black paint and wiped a thick streak under each eye and then another vertically down each cheek. Then he took a last dab of warpaint and made a symbol on the skin above his heart, three stroked lines like a stalk of wheat. Now the tin was useless as well, and he let it fall to the stream. It caught the current, floated a few feet, and then sank to the pebbles below, rippling in the sun like a holy Mayan agate, lost like a hundred tribes of gold.

Pulling out his combat knife Billy grasped the medicine bag around his neck and yanked it free. Then he twisted it around the hilt of the knife, binding the two together. He raised his head and closed his eyes as if in a trance and began a low mournful chant.

Schaefer and the others had been busy scrambling to the other side of the river, and they didn't notice that Billy had stayed behind consumed in ritual. The major labored up the opposite riverbank, Ramirez still on his back, before he turned and saw the Indian.

"Oh, Christ," he uttered. Then he shouted. "Billy!" But the Indian didn't hear a thing as he faced due north, the direction of the oncoming predator, knife raised like a holy sword. "Billy!" Schaefer called out again, but it was useless. Billy was as beyond the earth now as the alien.

The major hefted Ramirez higher onto his back and hauled up the hill. Anna waited at the top. Billy was crouching low now on the opposite bank, his knife extended in a fighting position.

Schaefer scrambled up the last of the slope, bringing

the wounded Ramirez to relative safety at the top of the
ridge overlooking the river. Just as he gently lowered
the Chicano to the ground and drew down his rifle he
heard a long piercing scream from the north bank of the
wide river. It was Billy Sole's final stand. The alien had
taken him in a flash, its weapon slicing through the Indian's jugular and then zigzagging down his chest and
belly like a mockery of some tribal blessing.

The loyal scout hadn't the ghost of a chance, armed
as he was with nothing more than a hunting knife and a
thousand faded years of Indian heritage. Schaefer spun
around helplessly at the sound of Billy's cry, too late
and too far away to help him. Ramirez, Billy's most
loyal friend, struggled to cock his rifle, but even as he
went through the motions he had an aching dread that
he'd never fight again.

Before the Chicano could release a single round the
alien's deadly weapon shot up the hill toward him like a
laser, the impact hurling him backward. The spearhead
lodged in his neck, pinning him to the ground as if he
were a butterfly frozen in a collector's display. Spouts of
blood gushed from the mortal wound—it seemed impossible he could still bleed after the grave wound he'd
received before—and his legs and arms twitched hideously in the seconds before death brought release.

In the melee Ramirez's MP-5 flew through the air
and landed at Anna's feet. Shocked yet stubbornly functional, she moved toward the rifle, as if some rebel instinct still fought to keep her alive. But the alien was
operating now at an inhuman pace—it could outdo in
action what a man could not even think to do. With
dazzling speed it roared uphill toward the girl, its livid
skin pulsating with glints of gold from the midday sun.
Seeing that Anna was going to land directly in the

alien's path, Schaefer spun about as she dived for the rifle. He lunged, kicking the weapon out of her reach to distract her, at the same time bellowing: "Run! Get to the chopper! Now!"

Then he opened fire at the onrushing monster, bullets flying everywhere, the barrel raking back and forth across the predator as Anna stumbled to her feet and ran for the jungle.

With a speed that all but made it a blur in Schaefer's eyes the predator attacked, hurling its weapon at the major with a wild triumphal shriek. The razor head of the spear sliced through the wooden stock of the gun, narrowly missing Schaefer's hand, severing the trigger guard and breech. Sparks flew as metal clashed on metal, steel on starstone.

With a last roar of adrenalin Schaefer took full combat command. "Stay low!" he ordered the fleeing girl, his last surviving commando. And as he scrambled for a defensive position himself he could feel the alien back away and turn to go downhill. But it wasn't fear, and it wasn't retreat. The major knew that the alien simply could take its own sweet time. It didn't need all its bodies at once. It was enjoying its earthling war and seemed to want to prolong the pleasure.

The alien tossed Ramirez's body aside as if it were a bag of trash. It was determined and focused now, all its otherworldly hunter's tactics and cunning raw and ready. The raging water posed no obstacle to the creature, and it sailed across like a hydroplane, barely breaking the surface even where it was five feet deep. As it arrived at the north bank of the river it churned up rocks and dirt with its spurs as it strode to Billy's body. It bent and began to pull the Indian apart, its narrow yellow optic nerve centers pulsing as it searched out the fading heat patterns of Billy's cooling organs.

Huddled among the rocks Schaefer only realized now that he'd been wounded. The force that had ripped the gun from his grip as the diamond head of the alien's spear shattered the rifle had gone on to slash deeply through Schaefer's shoulder, laying open the flesh almost to the bone. With his gun broken and useless, the major saw no alternative but to make a break down the canyon in the wake of the girl and run for his life.

Dutch wasn't accustomed to any sort of retreat, let alone running like a helpless fugitive headlong down a mountain, but he saw no other choice. Getting away was all he could think to do. Then if by some miracle he got clear, maybe he could buy a little time to regroup and make a final stab at fighting back. He barreled out of the rocks, ran through a tunnel of trees and past the sprung trap, and scrambled over the lip of the canyon and onto the steep downhill trail. He leaped over a fallen log, stumbled, struggled to his feet—running now on pure pounding adrenalin, his wounded shoulder oozing blood and stinging with a painful burn. His eyes were red and glazed with terror, he who had never feared anything in his life. Behind him he could hear the crunch of the alien's feet breaking twigs and crushing gravel as it jogged along in his wake.

Schaefer imagined that he could hear, almost feel the alien's heavy breath on him. The heat and panic and the steep trail had made him light-headed. He had to see how close the enemy was, so he turned his head without slowing his pace and saw the creature steadily bearing down the slope, Billy's heart and brain bloody in either hand. Schaefer had a wild desperate look of hope on his face as he saw a few more yards between them than he'd anticipated. Even as he turned back, ducking an overhanging limb and racing on, he didn't seem to realize that the alien was enjoying the chase—savoring the final confrontation with the leader.

As Schaefer felt the alien closing the space he ran like a madman, crazy to find a position from which to fight and knowing in his heart that the jungle would give no quarter to an unarmed man. He was losing ground and knew it. A shot of pain flashed through his shoulder, and for a moment he thought it was the alien's weapon entering him again. He looked up into the muggy birdless sky as if to rage a final goodbye to the world in which he had lived as a warrior.

Then by some queer glitch of fate the ground beneath him collapsed, and he disappeared from sight.

In a shower of leaves Schaefer crashed through the trees at a blind cliff edge, freefalling into space. He'd crossed an overhang of turf that looked secure but was only a thin layer of roots and moss that balanced above the canyon floor a hundred feet below. With a sickening crash he hit the top branches of a tall fir, then fell again through one canopy after another, desperately grabbing for limbs and branches to break his fall.

Finally he dropped to the floor layer of vegetation, his chest catching on the wide lower limb of a cottonwood, the impact knocking him near unconscious. Head whirling, vision blurred as if drugged, he teetered a few long agonizing seconds on the limb, then slid free, his numb fingers digging fruitlessly into the bark as he fell another ten feet to the swift churning river below.

He struggled to stay afloat, but the task was nearly impossible between the roar of the rapids and the weight of his soaked boots and clothing. As he was driven under by the force of the water he had the sudden lucid presence of mind to reach down and untie one boot, then the other, as he somersaulted along the savage bottom rocks. He kicked the boots free, and the thirty-pound advantage allowed him to struggle to the surface, where he ripped off his mottled shirt and pants and began to swim for shore, stroking furiously with his one good arm.

The alien peered over the edge of the cliff where Schaefer had fallen. It hesitated only a moment to lay aside the relics of the holy man. Then it dived over the edge as if it still harbored within it the glory of the hawk. It tore through the thick canopies of branches, agile and quick, bounding from limb to limb, soaring across twenty yards of space till it reached the low-hanging branch of a sycamore next to the river. It scanned the near jungle with its heat vision, seeking the telling yellow-red patterns that always revealed the frail form of man. But no man was there.

Schaefer was well downstream now, caught in a swirl of white water a mile from where the alien poised itself. As the major struggled toward shore he was helpless as a baby, totally at the mercy of cross currents and rapids which pulled him farther and farther till he was finally sucked into an undertow and hurled over a thirty-foot falls, plummeting down and driven deep underwater by the thundering force of the river.

Seconds later, in the wide pool at the base of the falls, the deafening explosion of currents was behind him. Schaefer rolled at the bottom of the pool, his mind spinning in confusion, unaware of where he was or how to reach air. By the last stroke of his luck the opposing currents gently propelled him to the surface, just in time to take a feeble breath. He was nearly finished, his energy sapped. But the surface water was sweet and reviving, and a few strokes with his good arm brought him into the shallows where he was at last able to grip his toes in the muddy riverbed.

As he tried to stand he pitched forward headlong into the gray muck by the riverbank. Then, with a final heave that drained the last shred of force he could muster, he crawled gasping and panting onto a sheltered mud overhang, settling into the tentacled root system of a dead tree, his body completely covered in thick gray sludge. He was fully primeval now, like the deepest beasts of the forest.

Nearly unconscious but still alert to his enemy, he raised his head and looked through glazed eyes to the opposite side of the river, scanning the bank. Seeing no sign of the alien he collapsed in relief, his eyes rolling up into his head as the waves of fatigue and pain took over. His last delirious thought was that he'd escaped, though just now in his battered state it was an escape that seemed strangely like death.

But the moment the major relaxed and was about to slip into unconsciousness he heard a shattering splash in the pool below the falls. The alien had leaped from the branches of an overhanging tree and landed on Schaefer's side of the river, throwing up a muddy wave that washed onto the major's feet. But even the reserve adrenalin was gone now. Dutch couldn't move a muscle as he saw the huge creature stand, water shimmering on its glowing body, its skin tone and texture swirling gray and brown and green in an attempt to match the surrounding river foliage. The glaring yellow orbs stared directly at the spot where Schaefer lay helplessly trapped in the tangle of roots.

As the predator surged forward, standing tall in the

shallows of the river, the major's last conscious thought was that he'd lost. All he could do was stare in horror and fear, paralyzed with shock and fatigue as the monster closed in on him. He waited for the sting of death, too exhausted to fight, defenseless and alone.

The alien rippled slowly through the water until only a few feet remained between them. Then it stopped, towering above, as if to inspect its prey for one last full moment before the annihilation. Images of Hawkins's, Blain's, and Davis's mangled bodies collided in Schaefer's mind as he lay there motionless, helpless. He closed his eyes to wait for the final blow, his dignity intact.

Seconds dragged by. Nothing. Schaefer dared open one muddy eye and saw the alien still standing as before, impatiently turning its head from left to right. It looked up and down the riverbank, back and forth among the tree roots, yet acted as if it didn't see him.

It didn't. It was trying to tune into Schaefer's heat source, but its optic scanning system couldn't penetrate the thick paste of cold mud that coated him. After a moment the creature uttered a skirl of irritation and bewilderment and turned aside. It moved heavily downstream from the battered Schaefer, searching the jungle clutches for its prey.

The major now opened his other eye as if to double-check what he saw with the first. He was speechless with disbelief. Staggered that he was still alive he watched the creature wander away, its prehensile spurs making a sucking sound in the mud. Then it rounded a bend and disappeared. Astonished and confused Schaefer tried to raise up on his elbows, but a sudden jab of pain in his shoulder caused him to collapse again.

He fell on his side and slipped into a troubled semi-coma, shivering now in the chill mud.

A minute later the slapping of helicopter blades grew louder over the top of the ridge. Then the steel bird flared into Schaefer's view as it followed the course of the river down the canyon. It maintained a holding pattern as a U.S. soldier leaned out the open side, scanning the riverbank with binoculars. Seeing no signs of life the chopper moved on, disappearing up the opposite rim of the canyon.

Anna ran and ran frantically through the jungle, her hair and clothes catching on brambles that ripped the coarse green cotton fatigues and bloodied her face. Her heart beat like a rabbit's from sheer exhaustion and panic as she gulped in great quantities of thick jungle air. She didn't have a breath left over to scream, and screaming was all that made any sense anymore. Her imagination was a kaleidoscope of blazing yellow eyes, and she felt the creature chasing her, reaching out a long three-fingered hand to grip her neck. But she kept on running, as if something far, far back had taught her to fight for even an hour more of life.

During the course of Schaefer's quaking paralysis he had a momentary nightmare in which the alien lanced him with its spearhead. The bleary-eyed mud-choked commando awoke abruptly and with a groan grappled up out of his swampy bed like some kind of being returned from the grave. He was hovering at the edge of delirium now, and his mind hammered with fantasies of the alien gorging his heart out. Then, still in an incoherent stupor, he swayed on his naked and bruised feet and began to stumble along the riverbank, slogging through mud like quicksand.

His shoulder flared with pain, and his temperature boiled at a hundred and three from the deep wound, the stress, and the chill of the mud. He lost his balance as he passed a clear shallow pool, staggering backward, suddenly finding himself waist-deep in the cool water. The soothing quiet shook him back to his senses, and his vision cleared. He stopped for a second to gather his wits. Then he waded over to the spongy moss-covered bank of the pool and sat down heavily, breathing slowly as if to recover his center of gravity.

The ripples he'd made on the water's surface as he pushed toward shore flattened now as he rested in the shallows. When the water calmed he noticed his shimmering reflection growing sharper and sharper, the waves of distortion gradually cohering into a true mirror image of his face and torso. His hair was matted flat with a thick coating of gray mud, and his face and chest were streaked with the pasty slate-colored sludge. He stared, mesmerized at his wild reflection. All the props of a soldier were gone.

Slowly, as if in a dream, he lifted his arm from the water and with his fingertips wiped clean a patch of skin along his cheek. He studied the sticky pungent mud on his hand, then looked back at the face in the water and saw the vivid contrast between the muddy camouflage and the lightly tanned skin beneath. As he stared, a wave of realization rushed over him so powerfully it dizzied him for a second.

"My God," he breathed aloud, his eyes widening with recognition. *"You couldn't see me!"* Awestruck he addressed the absent alien, each syllable crisp and precise, as if the insight were being engraved forever in his mind. Now he understood that the creature saw differently than the animals of earth. Maybe this could be its Achilles' heel. He chuckled almost hysterically, a combination of relief, exhausted tension, and the renewal of courage.

Schaefer gazed up into the failing light, at the treeline of the darkening forest, realizing fate had given him a second chance, an unexpected new weapon—his own chameleon challenge. The recognition of a possible defense stirred the commando in him. Vigorously he slapped up a handful of mud and carefully repainted the patches of skin he had earlier wiped clean.

"You couldn't see me," the major repeated with grinning delight, whispering the words this time as he stroked the side of his face with clay. His soldiering instincts quickened to life, the major's mind flared up like a stoked furnace, burning with ideas for a final combat.

The only weapon he still had left was his machete. His clothes, his shoes, everything had been lost to the rapids and falls. Naked now as the most primitive savage, he was stripped down to his instincts and wits and decided there was a certain irony to it all. He'd have to draw from the jungle now to build an arsenal with which to fight the creature. But the primitive twist didn't really disturb him, because all the high-tech fancy equipment the commandos had used thus far hadn't so much as made the creature flinch.

The newly charged warrior clambered out of the trench beside the pool, Olympian in size and with his coat of mud as ancient as a caveman. Immediately he set to work making a bow. First he carved magnesium shavings from a volcanic rock and swept them into a pile of kindling. Removing a dry match from the hollow handle of his knife—which also contained a coil of piano wire, a roll of green tape, and a couple of cyanide capsules—he lighted the shavings and watched them burn to a brilliant ice-white glow. Then he ripped a banana leaf from a nearby tree and sheltered the fire till the flame burned down in order to shield it from the alien's sensors. Gradually he fed the fire more kindling, fanning it rhythmically with the leaf.

Twenty minutes later he was twirling a seven-foot section of fire-hardened sapling between his feet and his good shoulder, scraping the char from the seasoned wood with his knife. Then he bent the bow and attached a long strand of piano wire to one end, carefully winding it for strength, using strips of green tape to cover the wire where the nock of the arrow would fit.

With fishing line he attached split parrot feathers to an arrow he'd whittled from a branch, its tip fashioned into a series of barbs, and rubbed it to a polished hardness against a smooth stone. Then he made three more just like it, methodically, one after the next. The arrows alone took him over an hour. But even as he lay the last of them neatly next to the others he knew he would have only one chance to win this battle—perhaps only one shot.

The sun disappeared behind the ridge of a dead volcano west of the Conta Mana border as Schaefer pounded a peeled root between two stones. He paused to drool saliva into the pulpy mass, scraping the milky substance onto a banana leaf. Mixing it with sticky sap from the banana tree he held it over the coals till the concoction began to steam. Then he opened the two cyanide capsules and tapped the powder into the bubbling liquid. He coated the arrow tips with the sticky poison, holding them over the coals so the sap bubbled and smoked as he spun the arrow in his hands, blowing steadily on the tips to cool and harden the mixture.

Using the blade of his machete he pried open the casing on one of the 40mm grenades that had washed ashore in his sodden gunbelt. Discarding the warhead, he dumped the dry propellant powder from the shell onto a leaf, mixing it with a mound of magnesium shavings. He opened the narrow, tight roll of gauze that had wrapped the cyanide capsules, fluffing it into a loose bundle the size of a golf ball, then poured the powder mixture over it, working it into the fabric.

Dutch was absolutely clear-headed now as he transferred the ball of explosive-laden gauze to a pliable dry leaf, closing it into a bundle and binding it at the top with a long strand of jungle grass. He twisted the remaining gauze around a match, leaving the head exposed, forming a self-striking fuse that he coated with sap. This too he thickly covered with powder from the grenade and poked the fuse into the leaf. Taking another blade of jungle grass he made a large loop, tied it about the grenade, and slipped the loop over his head.

Finally, using several sections of bamboo of different diameters, he fashioned a crude antipersonnel spear-bomb. The sharpened tongue of his belt buckle served as a firing pin, and a 40mm shell from his belt pouch as the explosive charge.

When he was done two hours later, Schaefer was a totally new kind of commando, outfitted by the natural guts of his planet. He would find out now which world was tougher, his own or the alien's. But as he slung his new-fashioned weapons about him and stood on the brink of the dark river, he had a pang of poignant memory for Billy. Whatever it was the Sioux had believed in, Schaefer was its last repository now. He was the only priest the world had left, this soldier of fortune who believed in nothing at all. And the poor defenseless planet was just going to have to make do with him.

SIXTEEN

A SAUCER-SHAPED MOON of heavy gold rose into the blackening sky as the last traces of a crimson-purple sunset liquefied into the Carribbean. In the dim light streaming from the early moon and late sun the silhouette of a lone, naked warrior appeared over a jagged ridge of rock. Dutch Schaefer was bathed in the gold of the moon on his left and the blood-red flickerings of the fading sun on his right. He had swathed his naked body entirely in clay and ochre, creating a mottled earthen camouflage pattern. He looked like an idol risen from a tomb. Holding his makeshift bow in one hand he moved up the canyon, ascending into a rising field of boulders like the fragments of a meteor.

The river below him flowed into a series of falls and pools, surrounded by massive table-top rocks, their crevices jammed with driftwood swept down at high water from forests above.

On a flattened section of the ridge Schaefer dragged a large tangle of branches into view, adding it to a growing mound of firewood. He knelt, tending to a pile of dried grass, leaves, and other tinder. Using the last of his precious matches he set a fire cupped in his hands, gently breathing and coaxing the tiny blaze into a slowly gathering fire, flames starting to lick upward through the dry pyre.

He stood now, staring into the rapidly growing blaze, turned and faced the canyon rim, raising his weapons high in one hand. From the depths of his blood a war cry burst, and as he threw back his head it rushed through his lungs and windpipe like a howl. It transcended time and worlds, primitive and visceral, as if from a wounded animal in a pain beyond pain.

The wail echoed for miles through the jungle canyons and silenced all the prowlers and night birds around him. It was the commando's beckoning invitation to the alien. His eyes flared in the yellow-orange glow of flames, and in that moment he looked unconquerable and terrifying, his mud-painted muscles tensed and ready.

The alien had retreated to its ship and was standing in the open doorway as Schaefer's echo came piercing through the trees within earshot. The cry was universally translatable—not just between peoples but between all worlds, wherever war had meaning. The creature craned its neck and lifted its head into the night looking like a wolf cussing the moon as it heard the cry and instantly understood its meaning. Instinctively it responded, but with a snakelike hiss that no one heard. Still, the seething noise boiling in its throat was an acceptance of Schaefer's call to battle.

It turned back into the ship, raising its weapon in one hand, while in the other it held a U-shaped sharpening device rather like a tuning fork. As the alien passed the tip of the weapon through the fork the spear that had slain all the other commandos flashed to life, emitting a deep harmonic hum as the blade glowed with energy, growing hotter and hotter with each stroke. The creature drew the now white-hot blade through the sharpener one last time, then lifted it to its golden eyes, studying its balance, the flashing alloy of the blade illuminating its humanoid face. The weapon meant something deeper than any mere object. To the alien it was a kind of extension of its will.

Emerging now from its interplanetary womb, the creature swung up to the tree line, climbing to the uppermost branches. It traveled silently from crown to crown, arriving at last at the canyon rim where far below it could see Schaefer's bonfire in the valley, the leaping, shifting, multicolored collage of heat waves and flares luring the alien onward, spellbound like a moth.

As the bait drew the predator, Schaefer hid back from the flames, tucked in a crevasse of rock and broken tree stumps on the slope above the bonfire. His eyes shifted trancelike, moving from side to side, watching the approaches to the fire below. His senses were alert, his nerves on a wire edge.

The alien began its descent, its shadow-form descending through the canyon, a rippling movement of grays and blacks passing across the shifting light patterns on the canyon walls cast by the growing flames below. Its golden eyes probed the canyon, hungry to get closer to the swirling patterns of heat thrown off by the gaseous flames of the bonfire.

Schaefer sat motionless in an Indian crouch, waiting for destiny to arrive, nearly invisible in his mud camouflage, one with the darkness of the trees and rocks. Suddenly, all around him, he noticed the buzz and click of insects and the croak of frogs had stopped. He immediately recognized this as a sign of the alien's presence, for he'd come to understand that all creatures sensed and feared the invader.

Schaefer drew his makeshift bow to full arch, his wounded shoulder trembling, the blood beginning to seep through the bandage again from the muscle strain. With the bow at full draw he stared intently, concentrating, searching for the alien's iridescent form in the dancing light below.

Then, like a giant insect, it dropped from above, rocketing down as if from the sky, its steellike spurs digging deep into a tree stump.

Schaefer froze at the sound, his mud-rimmed eyes wide with fascination and fear. He couldn't tell how far away the creature was in the darkness—maybe fifty, seventy-five feet. The major knew that the slightest movement on his part would bring on an instant attack, so he waited as still as a stump himself. At that moment he felt a weird comfort to know he was more at one with the jungle than his enemy.

Enticed by the heat patterns vibrating from the fire and lacing into the canyon darkness, the alien dropped another thirty feet closer to the flaming lure. It raised its weapon, still white as steel newly tempered, like a mythic warrior's sword. The yellow optic cells glittered like a honeycomb in the reflection from the fire as the alien looked around slowly. The quiet hissing sound escaped from its tensed mouth like a burning fuse, an instinctive signal that it was in a battle mode.

As Schaefer squatted motionless and rigid he heard the low thump of the alien's feet landing on a nearby

table rock. Swift and silent the major turned and fired a
poison arrow at the sound. It zipped through the darkness, and an instant later he heard the telling thud as the
tip lodged in the trunk of a tree. "Shit!" muttered Dutch,
berating himself for wasting a shot and for betraying his
presence. The arrow had missed the alien's bulbous
head by inches.

The predator was as quick to strike back. Its arm
whipped so fast it was only a blur in the fire-shot night
as it activated its weapon, the projectile streaking downward and exploding into a log so close to the major's leg
he could feel the wind. The impact sent up a shower of
wood chips into the night.

It was like a terminal game of chess now, and once
again it was Schaefer's move. He clutched his makeshift
weapons, leaping from boulder to boulder as he fled the
vulnerable spot. He jumped down into the clearing near
the fire, landing hard, rolling out of the light and into
the protective shadows of the rocks on the far side. Now
the roaring bonfire lay between man and alien like a
sacred zone of death and regeneration.

Schaefer glanced around and saw that he was in a
sort of natural amphitheater formed by the sheer walls
of rock that shot up a hundred feet behind him into the
black night sky. Shadows cast by the fire danced eerily
across the rough stone, till Schaefer was almost certain
he could see the outline of painted forms, and ancient
glyphs incised into the stone.

As the major positioned himself under the protective
overhang of a jut of rock he found himself in a small
space protected on three sides. He crouched with his
bow and felt the pain scream across his shoulder. The
wound was spilling blood freely again, and as he

watched it drip on the stony ground he could see broken
pieces of pottery and the carved head of a jaguar that
looked like jade in the dancing firelight. But he didn't
have a minute to root around for treasure. For all he
knew these fragments would mark his grave.

Then, above on the rocky plateau, the silhouette of
the alien appeared for a single moment. It looked victorious and huge against the sky, its form revealed in the
play of the flames. It moved now down the rocky wall,
gliding in and out of the darkness like a serpent as the
rocks would now and then shelter it from the orange
glow.

As the creature crept slowly downward, nearer and
nearer to the light, Schaefer distinguished a new sound
over the crackle and sputter of the fire and the rushing
river far below—a sound that brought fear and a savage
determination to his heart. It was the rhythmic scraping
of the alien's hard, tusklike foot spurs, screeching like
chalk on a blackboard. The major rose slowly to his
feet, slung another arrow in his bowstring, and drew
back on it as he moved out of his shelter and around a
large boulder, heading toward the scraping sound.

They were only feet from each other now. The creature paused erect in the strobing light, craning its head
and slowly turning as it tried to orient itself to the diver-
sity of sounds. The circular walls of the rocky amphitheater richocheted everything, throwing its delicate
radar off. Fortunately for the major, the variable light
rendered the alien's optic nerve centers dull and dim as
it moved among the inert forms of the rocks. It beheld a
world of soft, ill-defined shapes in a pale magenta field
of flickering heat.

Schaefer crept forward, placing one foot in front of

the other with all the stealth and skill of a Sioux scout. Suddenly he would stop and strain to listen, trying to place the direction of the frightening scrape of the alien's spurs. The sound reverberated off the granite walls, so he couldn't pin it down enough to fire at it. Nervously he looked around in a full circle, uncertain where to move next. Then, unbelievably, he heard the whisper of a human voice softly echoing among the rocks. It was Anna. "Look out . . . behind you," came the warning, almost seductive in its intimacy.

Schaefer spun about, his breath catching as the words drifted to him. Wide-eyed and straining every tendon and muscle he waited for the voice again but heard nothing—just the distant muted flow of the river and the hissing and popping of the dying fire above. As the flames dwindled, the shadows grew longer and darker with every minute.

Then Anna's voice again. "Look out, Major . . . behind you!"

Schaefer swiveled in place. "Anna?" he whispered back. It was almost pathetic, the need he felt just then to make contact with somebody human. Trancelike, he moved toward the sound.

In a shallow cave among the rocks, not more than twenty feet from Schaefer, the alien mimicked the girl again. "Over here. I know the way out!"

Numbly Schaefer followed the bait, closer and closer. But as he moved in a kind of dream state something made him pause at the sound of *more* familiar voices. "Dillon, over here," came the voice of Mac, and Mac was dead.

Bolting awake with horror Schaefer backed quickly into a narrow tuck between a boulder and the high sheer wall of the amphitheater. His feet moved lightly as he went into a bowman's crouch, the shadow-light deepening with the dying fire above, till he almost seemed like something ancient painted on the rock. Bow drawn, trapped against the rock, he heard the scraping sound of the predator once again. The noise came from the right, then shifted back to the left, then right again. The major didn't know where to shoot and began to sweat with panic.

It was time for more desperate weapons. The major withdrew the flash-grenade from around his neck. Then, with a swift jerk of his hand, he struck and tossed it forward, and it exploded, briefly illuminating the whole area below the bonfire. During that instant Schaefer saw his enemy poised on a rock above him, its weapon raised and about to strike. But momentarily blinded by the flash the alien recoiled, ducking its head to the side.

As the phosphorous shed by the grenade faded Schaefer seized the advantage. Before the golden eyes could activate again he hurled his bang-stick spear. It smashed into the boulder at the creature's feet and detonated, exploding the face of the rock. The alien sprang back too late, and shrapnel tore into its body. With a terrifying scream of pain and fury the creature clutched frantically at its neck and chest. Then with a second bloodcurdling shriek of rage it jumped off its rocky platform and disappeared into the night.

Cascades of water surged over an eight-foot drop in the river's rocky bed as it coursed through the ravine, throwing up a perpetual mist. Schaefer, his bow still drawn, followed the weird trail of the alien's luminous amber blood as it dripped from the fresh wounds. As the major ducked behind the falls, the mist sprayed him, washing off some of his clay camouflage. Fixated, he followed the trail like a starving panther on the scent of a plump boar. Schaefer's own shoulder bled freely down his arm and side, and the crimson mixed with the gray streaks of clay still clinging to his torso. Oblivious now to the searing pain in his shoulder he took in huge hot gulps of air, his eyes wide and glowing with vengeance. He looked with relish at an amber glob of alien blood beaded like gum on a bamboo shoot.

"Bleed, you bastard," he hissed angrily.

The major flexed his bow, testing its vital tension, then resumed his tracking. He followed the luminous blood trail across the ledge where a huge vertical boulder had shifted in an earthquake. There the trail ended abruptly. No more sign of the viscous amber ooze. Schaefer took another step forward across a darkened alcove and spun quickly as he felt the alien springing to action out of the shadows.

The major faced his enemy hand-to-hand at last, savagely kicking out at the creature's arm. The spear that had killed so many flew from its grip and clattered to the rocks below. Before it could quite recover, its golden eyes blinking bewilderedly, Schaefer followed with a karate kick to the chest, hurling the creature face forward onto the ground, its broad back exposed to the veteran commando. Instantly Schaefer was standing over the alien, his bow drawn and poised, the blood from his shoulder dripping onto the creature's livid skin.

Slowly the alien rolled onto its back, revealing its ghastly face. Its eyes were bleached nearly white with shock from the loss of blood. Its body rippled out of control as it tried desperately to disappear into its dark surroundings—the old chameleon's escape—but now in its weakened state it couldn't bring off the transformation.

The major's curiosity exploded. "Who the hell are you?" he demanded, glaring down, his own eyes blazing deep in their sockets. He was monstrous in his own way.

Incomprehensible sounds choked and coughed from the alien's gullet till at last it began to form words. At first they crackled as if they were coming through a weak radio signal. Then they got clearer and stronger with each syllable until the alien did a perfect imitation of Schaefer's voice. "Who...the...hell...are... you?" it mimicked slowly, methodically, almost in singsong.

Then it collapsed for a moment as if it were totally spent of energy. But with a single concentrated thrust it lashed out an arm, activating the razor-sharp spurs at its wrists. An instant later it coiled a leg and kicked upward with renewed and brutal strength, its terrible heel spur ripping into Schaefer's thigh, hurling him backward so that he crashed into a shallow ditch of water. Floundering desperately the major grabbed for his bow, which had bounced away in the fall. He found it just as the creature rose to its feet, inhaling deeply and hungrily, gaining strength again with every breath.

Schaefer saw the alien retrieve and raise its weapon again. Then, with one instinctive movement, his shoulder throbbing with pain, he drew the arrow back to its tip and let it fly. With a deadly thud it penetrated deeply into the alien's neck. Another bloodcurdling scream of rage echoed through the trees as the enemy clutched its throat, dropping its spear once more. A second later it bounded away down the rocks, hissing and rumbling with pain and loss and anger.

Schaefer scrambled out of the water and pursued, following the bowl of the canyon above the river as he picked up a fresh trail of the faintly luminous amber.

The major's shoulder had stopped bleeding, leaving a caked clot of thickened blood along the gash. But his thigh was streaming blood profusely, and with every step a hot stab of pain shot through his leg. Yet he pushed onward, half hobbling, climbing the slope by swinging the weight to his good leg. The trail was clear to follow because the alien was too weak to sail through the treetops or clone itself into a creature of flight, bird or fly or wisp of air. It stumbled along through the tangled forest, leaving a swath of trampled grass, broken twigs and chunks of dirt thrown up by its dragging spurs.

Spent and enraged, groaning with fury, the alien arrived at the edge of the clearing where its ship waited. It was bleeding severely now and had lost virtually all of its camouflage abilities. Its skin had turned a pale sickly green and slithered along its body like a snake struggling to shed itself. With trembling three-pronged hands it grasped the shaft of the arrow protruding from its neck and pulled it out with a roar of pain. A spurt of gray choke from deep in its guts erupted and spilled from its mouth and down its leathery chin.

Schaefer was relentless in pursuit, obsessed with ending the killer's rampage. He was working his way through a narrow passageway in a grove of rubber trees when he almost walked into a vast spider web that measured four feet across, blocking the path. Instinctively he moved to sweep it aside with his machete when he noticed an odd quality about the way it caught the moon's dim light. Examining more closely he saw that the network of membranes wasn't the silken threads of an insect at all, but hair-fine wire—a trap.

He jumped back at the realization, then picked up a hefty branch, hurled it into the center of the trap, and watched the mechanism spring into action. There was a metallic snap followed by a high-pitched whine as the wood impacted on metal. The branch, five inches around, was violently torn apart, and pieces of wood flew in opposite directions, whipping into the jungle.

Schaefer wiped his brow with relief, then pushed ahead, stepping gingerly over the coils of wire lying inert on the ground. He didn't even stop to wonder if this was part of the guerrillas' or the alien's arsenal. The death snares were so all-encompassing now that they seemed to be set by the violent earth itself.

A few minutes later he arrived close enough to the alien ship to see the surreal blue glow filtering through the trees. Then, in the clearing ahead, he spied the alien itself, staggering toward the light. Schaefer was about to close the distance and have it out at last, when he was stopped in his tracks by a hideous sight that came crashing down on his senses, obliterating everything else.

At one end of the clearing, translucent human skins had been stretched over wooden frames, the attached scalps rippling lightly in the breeze. Flayed bodies, some lying on the open ground, were scattered about the area, while others hung from the trees in much the way Davis and his men were found. There must have been at least thirty bodies, guerrillas as well as commandos.

"Even the fuckin' Nazis didn't do this," Schaefer muttered in outrage, sick at the pit of his stomach like one of the men who'd liberated Buchenwald.

But he had no time to sink into the horror, so he forced his mind to be tempted only by the rage, and used that rage to drive him forward. He turned again to his target and saw that the alien was passing through the shimmering glow of the force field. Cautiously Schaefer walked closer and saw the egg-shaped outline of the ship. The creature was walking with great difficulty up the ramp toward the open door of the spacecraft. It still looked awesome as its silhouette was bathed in the pulsing blue glow of the ship, but to Schaefer in his fury the creature seemed more frightened than frightening.

Weakened though he was by his wounds and by exhaustion, Schaefer staggered forward and looked up in time to see the alien wave a hand across a light beam. The ship instantly responded with a turbine whine which built slowly and steadily in volume and pitch. The predator turned and gazed out over the thick jungle that still hid Schaefer, as if it sensed the commando's presence in the shadows. Then it turned back and entered the force field. The door began to slowly close, as if it sensed its captain was about to enter and there was no time to spare.

Schaefer felt a sudden throb of panic as he saw the enemy about to retreat to safety. He darted into the clearing and spotted the alien's weapon at the foot of the ramp. The creature had either dropped it in the delirium of its wounds, or perhaps it felt no need for the power any more. It was on its way home now. There would be other weapons for other planets.

Schaefer grabbed up the odd instrument, perplexed. How to operate it? Was it keyed to something in the creature itself so that only the alien could fire it? The major squeezed the handle and felt resistance. Again he tried with the last ounce of his strength and screamed a bellow of rage as he crushed down on the handle. Sud-

denly a blue-white light shot out at the end, and the
spear was activated. Schaefer raised it, sensing its
power and function by sheer feel, warrior to warrior. He
leveled the thing at the disappearing back of the alien
just as the door was closing behind it. Schaefer shouted
triumphantly and hurled it.

Flaring with deadly energy the weapon shot off like a
meteor up the laser ramp, accelerating through the door
and into the spacecraft. It lodged in the back of the
creature's neck, and in that instant the door froze half-
open. The alien's head exploded but slowly, in a kind of
slow motion, almost as if the gravity within the craft
was different from the earth's. A geyser of amber-
orange blood shot out, then pale green tissue as the
brain burst. Then the spearhead continued out through
the alien's throat, burying itself in the side of the ship,
sending bolts of plasma-energy arcing through the force
field.

Schaefer fell forward onto the ground, half in a
swoon as he stared at the incredible sight. The whirring
sound from the ship grew to a feverishly high ear-
splitting pitch, and the whole craft began to tremble and
quiver as if it too would explode. But by now Schaefer
could no longer tell if he was conscious or unconscious.
He wasn't sure any more if he was still in one piece
himself.

Two attack helicopters' blades slapped the thick jungle air as they powered their way through the canyon,
racing along at treetop height. The first carried a VIP
crew. Its leader, General Phillips, turned to his most
important passenger, the rebel Anna Gonsalves.

"Does this look familiar?" he demanded, pointing to
the snaking river below.

She peered down at the dimly lit tangle of jungle and rushing water and the bramble-covered ridge. Then she saw the huge mahogany log lying beached against the shore—the log on which she and Schaefer and Ramirez had crossed the churning rapids. "Yes . . . yes!" she said, nodding enthusiastically. "Right down there." And she pointed to the rocky ridge. "That's where I saw him last."

Phillips turned to the pilot. "Follow that ridge," he ordered. As the pilot tried to oblige, maneuvering quickly in the canyon updrafts, his instrument panel went wild, the gauges spinning, digital readouts out of control. The pilot lurched forward over the steering lever, desperately fighting to regain their equilibrium.

At the same moment the chopper went out of control, the alien's ship had reached a loud deafening whine, and the ground in the clearing around it began to quake. Schaefer, realizing even in his half-stupor that the thing was going to explode, ignored his knifing pains and ran desperately for the jungle, seeking cover. He sprinted to the edge of the clearing and dived over the embankment just as a blinding purple flash blew the ship to pieces. Fragments of the rare interplanetary metals shot hundreds of feet into the sky. A half mile away the choppers were enveloped in the flash of intense light and momentarily helpless. The aftershock pulsed through the sky like a sonic boom, knocking the choppers haywire as they floundered two hundred feet in the air.

Below, concentric waves of energy pulsed outward from the center of the blast as if a miniature star were being born.

Then, just at the moment when they would have

dropped like birds with broken wings to the trees below, the choppers' mechanisms returned to normal function as the sonic wave subsided. The pilots were just able to pull up in time to prevent crashdown.

"Holy mother o' Jesus!" Phillips's pilot exclaimed.

The general was shaken and totally bewildered by the bomb blast, but he had to stay in charge. He knew something extraordinary had just happened and that it was beyond the soldiering techniques of the guerrillas or even his own beloved army. "Orbit right," he ordered. "Check out ground zero!"

The pilot leveled the craft and headed across the treetops toward the source of the blast, now rolling with smoke as several trees went up like fireballs.

Meanwhile, Schaefer cautiously lifted his head from the ground where he'd flattened himself in the dirt for protection. He stared at the devastation with a curious dispassion. The entire area was deadened—every leaf, every tree, every living thing within fifty feet of the ship was black and charred, stripped down to a pulp of smoldering wood and naked dirt. And everything was coated with a fine sifting of white ash, like fallout after a nuclear blast. At the center site of the ship itself magnesium flares still burned with exotic colors, like some weird carnival at the end of the world. Schaefer rose up from his depression and stared hollow-eyed. Behind him the sound of choppers grew louder as the two craft flared over the trees, but the major didn't appear to notice.

The crews gaped at the devastation as they approached slowly, their eyes struggling to penetrate the dense white smoke. As one descended the other hovered a hundred feet above. As the first drew closer to the ground its propwash created a whirling storm of white dust. As they hovered about twenty feet over the annihilated landscape and some of the dust blew off, they beheld a figure materialize from the raging smoke and ash, a naked body covered head to toe in mud, blood, and soot. It was Schaefer, but looking for all the world as if *he* were the alien.

As the chopper hovered over the blast site where the spacecraft once had stood pristine, the visored and helmeted men with weapons poised looked suspiciously at Schaefer. To the lone naked warrior gazing up at the choppers like a caveman the soldiers looked as much like aliens to him as he to them. Which was the truer soldier? Who could say any more? All the rules had changed, though only the naked man knew how much.

The door gunner swung his M-60 into firing position, pointing it directly at Schaefer. He racked the bolt, loading a round. The other three soldiers watched silently, tensed, frightened. Schaefer didn't look human at all. They didn't know who he was. But Anna, crouching beside the door gunner, staring transfixed at the strange creature before her, narrowed her eyes and tilted her head. There was something about his gait, about the lift of his broad shoulders, that looked familiar.

As more of the ash settled like snow, Schaefer's image grew clearer. He looked up dazed and raised a hand, like a lost man in space making contact with members of an alien race for the first time. Men were looking at men, but neither side seemed to know anymore what a man was. It was a hopeless standoff.

The chopper hovered nearer to the ground now but still as if reluctant to land. More helmeted and visored men crowded at the door, more weapons leveled at

Schaefer. Suddenly Anna's eyes went wide with recognition. She held up her own hand, like a mirror image of the waving man below, and shouted: *"No! No!* Don't shoot!" And she shoved the gunner's rifle aside just as he squeezed the trigger, so the weapon shot off harmlessly into the smoking trees.

"What is it?" Phillips demanded, grabbing the woman's hand as if he feared she was sending signals.

"It's your man!" Anna said excitedly, pointing down at the major. "It's him!"

Phillips squinted and looked hard. "Holy shit, so it is. Hold your fire!" he bellowed.

Anna shoved her way through the huddle of men and leaped from the craft, which was hovering about five feet above the ground. She landed on her knees on the ruined ground below, scrambled to her feet, and charged toward Schaefer screaming, tears streaming down her cheeks. "You're alive!" she hollered, then threw her head up to the sky. "Thank you, Father—he's alive!"

And she rushed over to the dazed, shocked commando, tottering there in the war-torn clearing and barely able to stand. She threw her arms around him. "Oh, thank God you're alive," she sobbed, impulsively covering his bloody chest with kisses.

Schaefer looked down at her through glazed eyes, then his mouth turned up with a faint smile of recognition. He let her take his hand and lead him over to the chopper, which now hugged the ground, its blades slowly whirling. The soldiers all stood back from the door as Anna scrambled in and reached for the major. He gripped her hand and, grunting with his wounds, slung himself up and in. For a moment there as he was in movement he showed a trace of the old football hero,

victorious at game's end and ready to be borne from the
stadium on the shoulders of his teammates.

Moments later they were airborne, heading at high
speed across the trackless jungle, the rotors thumping
like heavy machine-gun fire. Schaefer was seated on a
bench in the cargo hold beside Anna, who still clutched
his hand and wept softly, though she was smiling the
whole time. A green army blanket was thrown about the
major's shoulders, mud and blood still streaked all over
him. His entire body seemed laced with deep cuts.

The medic, hunched before him with an open field
kit, syringe, and bandages, turned to Phillips. "Looks
like he's been through hell. I can't believe he's still
alive. What the fuck went on down there?"

"If it hadn't been for her he'd be dead now," Phillips
retorted, glancing down at Anna, confused in his heart
because he knew she was a rebel. "That story she told
us, I still can't believe it."

The general looked directly into Anna's eyes, as if to
check once more about her incredible explanation. She
returned a defiant look, even through her tears, that said
she had been through hell herself, that all of it was real.
Then she looked to Schaefer, as if there was comfort at
least in sharing the secret, as if feeling a bond with the
commando would prove to herself she wasn't crazy.
And somehow she knew they would also share more,
now they were no longer enemies and the nightmare
was safely past.

Schaefer looked back at her and smiled wearily. His
eyes were a little clearer now, and his breathing had
calmed. Then he turned to look out at the bright gold of
the rising sun as the two choppers headed off for the far
horizon. For a moment he seemed to stare deep into the

distant heavens, but what he saw didn't register in his hooded eyes. He had had his private war, and the winning of it, and whatever peace it left behind, were things he would never speak. It was a kind of homage to the men he'd lost. As he stared at the sky hints of pink and gold splashed across the Conta Mana border, announcing the coming of day.